Ryker

SAN FRANCISCO SHOCKWAVES
BOOK ONE

SAMANTHA LIND

SAMANTHALIND.COM

Ryker
San Francisco Shockwaves Book 1
Copyright 2022 Samantha Lind
All rights reserved

Paperback ISBN: 978-1-956970-07-4
Special Edition ISBN: 978-1-956970-19-7

Cover Design by Y'All That Graphic
Editing by *Amy Briggs ~ Briggs Consulting LLC*
Proofreading by *Proof Before You Publish*

❀ Created with Vellum

Contents

CHAPTER 1

Ryker

JUNE

TODAY IS A NEW DAY. I roll out of bed, stretching as the sun peeks through the curtains of my bedroom window. It's a new summer, which means it's a new two-bedroom apartment I'm calling home for the few months I have off between seasons. I crave time with my daughter. I've missed so much of her life living on the other side of the country and due to my travel schedule. It isn't like she's ever been able to come live with me.

Today is also the day I find out if my life is changing again. While I signed a multi-year contract last summer with the Indianapolis Eagles, they, unfortunately, couldn't protect me in today's expansion draft. While some players wouldn't be excited about the prospect of being picked up by a new team in the league, I'm hoping they do pick me. It's my shot to live and work in the same city as my daughter. It's my shot to put down some roots somewhere, hopefully until I'm ready to retire in another few seasons.

I grab a quick shower before pulling on some athletic shorts and a hockey T-shirt. I'm picking up Ellie in an hour, and I want to be ready for her. I'm sure her first request will be to stop at the mall or some store. She's always conning me into buying her whatever her mom says no to. I've always made sure they have enough money to have a roof over their heads, food in the kitchen, and any clothing or school items Ellie needs. Just because Michelle and I aren't together doesn't mean my daughter needs to suffer.

"Hi, Ryker," Michelle greets when she opens the door. "Ellie will be right out; she was just packing a few more things."

"Hey, how are things around here?" I ask.

"They're good. Can you give me a call when she's not around or is ignoring you? I wanted to discuss something with you."

"Sure, everything okay?" I ask.

"Yeah," she says, but the way she's biting the bottom edge of her lip tells me otherwise. She's either nervous to tell me something, or there's a problem.

"Hey, Dad!" Ellie interrupts as she comes bouncing into the room.

"Hey, Ellie Bean." I pull her into a huge hug. "Missed you," I say into her hair. I still can't believe she's gotten so big.

"Missed you, too, Dad." She squeezes me back.

"Shall we get going?" I ask.

"Yes," she answers me before saying goodbye to her mother. I don't miss the fact Michelle seems to hug her a little tighter than usual, but maybe I'm just reading into things a little too deep.

"I'll call you later," I say before heading out.

"Can we go out for lunch?" Ellie asks once we're in the car and ready to pull out of the driveway.

"I suppose. Where do you want to go?"

"I don't care; Mom just keeps saying no to eating out, and I'm tired of making sandwiches all the time."

"Everything okay at home?" I pry.

"Mom's been weird lately. I think she's hiding something from me," Ellie says as she stares out the window.

"She asked me to call her when you're not around," I tell my daughter. "I think you might be on to something, but I'll get to the bottom of it."

"How about the food court at the mall?" Ellie asks.

I chuckle, knowing a trip to the mall would happen. "Sure." I agree to her request.

"What's so funny?" she asks, turning her attention my way.

"I thought to myself this morning you'd find a way to convince me to take you to the mall at some point this week. It didn't take you long, at all." I laugh some more before I take the on-ramp for the highway.

I walk around the mall with my daughter, constantly checking my phone for a call or text from my agent. I'm hoping to hear sooner than later so I know what the future holds.

"Dad, *Dad!*" Ellie calls to me. I pop my head up to where she stands, looking at a display rack with new iPhones. "Can you upgrade my phone?" She bats her eyelashes at me, and I can feel all my badassery slipping through my fingers. If the guys I face off with on the ice, night after night, knew just how wrapped around my daughter's finger I was, they'd have a field day roasting me right into the ice.

"How old is your current one?" I ask.

"Like, two years or so. The battery sucks on it, and it dies on me all the time; then Mom gets pissed because she can't reach me until I can get it plugged in and recharged. A new phone would stop that from happening," she pleads her case.

"How much for the new one?" I ask the salesperson standing behind the display.

"That depends on the model and size," the salesgirl says.

"Do you know what one you want?" I ask Ellie.

"Of course!" she says excitedly.

Twelve hundred dollars later, I walk out of the store, my daughter on cloud nine, as we make our way to the food court to grab some lunch.

I set the tray with my burger and fries on the table, then grab my phone from my pocket when it rings. My agent Bruce's face flashes across the screen, and I answer immediately.

"Hey, Bruce," I greet as I answer his call.

"Ryker, how are you?" he asks.

"Just fine, even if I did just drop over a grand on my daughter's new phone."

"Ah, the joys of kids." He laughs.

"She's lucky I love her," I tell him as I look at my daughter, who's geeking out over her new phone.

"I've got some news. San Francisco has taken you in the expansion draft. You're the first official member of the Shockwaves. Congratulations, Ryker. We finally got you onto a team in California."

"Wow," I say. Even though I knew this was a possibility, it still hits me. I'll get to see my daughter regularly. She'll see me play at home if she chooses to attend my games. Everything I've wanted is finally—*finally*—falling into place.

> Are you free? Ellie is asleep, and I'm free to talk.

> Give me five, and I'll give you a call back. Is that okay?

> Works for me.

I TOSS my cell on the cushion next to me. I have no idea what Michelle might need to talk to me about. After spending the afternoon and evening with Ellie, she's her usual happy self.

My phone rings and vibrates next to me, so I quickly grab it and answer the call.

"Hey, Michelle," I greet.

"Hi, Ryker. How was today?" she asks.

"It was good, even if she did con me into a bunch of shit at the mall." I chuckle, thinking back to our trip. I sometimes overcompensate for the amount of time I have to be away from Ellie by buying her stuff. I know items can never replace being in her life, but we've made do with what time we get.

"Oh lord, I can only imagine what she convinced you of today. She already texted me about the new phone, which she did kind of need. Her old one has been acting up; I just hadn't gotten around to upgrading her."

"She said you'd approve, and she's a good kid. I don't mind spoiling her every once in a while. It's only money; I can't take it with me when I die.

Enough about our shopping trip; what did you need to talk to me about?" I ask, not wanting to beat around the bush any longer.

"First, congratulations on the trade; I know you've been trying to get out to a western team."

"Thanks. It's still sinking in I'll not only be on the West Coast but close enough to see Ellie regularly."

"Yeah," she nervously laughs. "That's what I need to talk to you about. I've been offered a major promotion, but it requires me to relocate and travel for work about fifty percent of the time."

"Where do you have to move to?" I ask, and dread fills my chest.

"Dallas," she says, and I can hear her nervousness. "But I have an idea," she's quick to add. "Ellie is fifteen, and this is the only place she's known as her home. What if we let her decide if she wants to stay here in California and move in with you full-time, or move with me to Texas?"

"I'd be on board with that. After the news today, I was going to start looking for a more permanent place to rent or buy, since it looks like I'll be here in California for the foreseeable future. If she's going to be living with me full-time, I'll need a comfortable place for that arrangement."

"Well, that went a lot better than I expected," she says, and I can hear the air escape her lips through the phone.

"Have you said anything to Ellie? She said you've

been acting weird lately, and she didn't know what was going on. I think she's worried you're sick or something."

"Oh shit, I'll call her tomorrow and tell her everything. I feel horrible knowing she thought it was something like that. I was just worried she'd be mad about having to leave her friends."

"She might still choose to do that; she's only used to seeing me for small bits of time; she might not want to move in with me and be away from you for a change," I state, secretly hoping she doesn't decide to leave. I was looking forward to the day I'd make it to California and be around her more than I have been for the last fifteen years.

"I guess we'll know for sure tomorrow or in the coming weeks," Michelle states.

"When will you need to move?" I ask.

"Ideally, they'd like me there in the next couple of weeks, but are willing to work with me if I need more time to wrap things up here before I can make it out."

"Well, if it helps, I've got Ellie covered. Even if it's just for the rest of the summer. "

"Thanks, Ryker. I appreciate it and how you're so chill about this. I was apprehensive, especially after today's news."

"I won't lie, it will suck if she wants to move with you, and I'm right back in the situation I've been in her entire life, but I also won't fault her or you for that happening. You're her default parent, and it will be a complete life change to be away from you and with me full-time. If she does decide to stay here, I'll need to find someone who can stay with her when I'm on the road, but that's a bridge we can cross when the time comes."

"She might be able to stay with a friend some of those times," Michelle suggests.

"That's an idea, but some of our road trips can be over a week long, and often. That's a lot to ask of someone."

"I'm sure you'll figure it out. Before we panic about it, let's see what she says tomorrow, and we can go from there."

"Sounds good. Congratulations on the promotion, by the way."

"Thanks, I've been working my ass off, and it's nice to be recognized for it, finally."

"ELLIE, IT'S TIME TO GO," I call out. We're meeting Michelle for lunch. We decided to tell her about Michelle's new job and give her the choice together.

"Yeah, where are we going?" she asks as she stops in front of me, securing her hair into a ponytail. I still sometimes get choked up at just how grown up she is these days.

"Meeting your mom for lunch at PF Chang's."

"Oh, yum. I haven't been there in forever."

"Let's get going, then, we're supposed to meet her in twenty minutes."

I follow her out of the apartment and down to my car. Ellie is engrossed in her phone on the drive over; the silence between us does not seem to bother her.

"Hi," Michelle greets us when we enter the restaurant. "It should only be a few more minutes before they seat us," she says.

"Hey, Mom," Ellie greets her as she walks into Michelle's open arms.

"Are you having a good time with your dad?" Michelle asks her.

"Yep, want to see my new phone?" she asks as she holds out the newest iPhone.

"Michelle, party of three," the hostess calls out and we all step her way. She shows us to our booth, and I wait while Ellie and Michelle both slide in. We're seated at a U-shaped table, with Ellie in the middle of us. "Your server will be right with you," the young woman says before leaving us to look over the menus.

It doesn't take long for our server to approach and take our drink and food orders. While we wait for our appetizers to come out, I jump right to the point of this lunch date.

I start out by saying, "Ellie Bean, your mom and I have something we need to talk to you about."

"Are you dying?" she blurts out, looking at her mother.

"Gosh, no, did you really think I was?" Michelle asks, her hand pressed to her chest. The panicked look on her face also tells me she didn't expect Ellie to ask that.

"You've been kind of weird, lately, and then for Dad to spring this lunch on me, I figured something was up. You two aren't getting together, are you?" she asks, now.

"Nope, we're not getting together." I chuckle at the thought.

"I'm not sick and your dad and I aren't together, but I do have some news," Michelle says. "I was offered a promotion at work—" she starts to say.

"That's awesome, Mom!" Ellie interrupts, leaning over to give her mom a side hug.

"It is, thank you, but there's more," Michelle says. "The promotion requires me to move to Texas and requires a fair amount of travel."

"We're moving?" Ellie asks, a tremble in her voice.

"Maybe," I chime in. "That's the second part of what we have to tell you. Your mom and I decided that we'd give you the choice. You're old enough to make some decisions, and now that I'll be here, if you want to stay in California, you can move in with me.

You can take a few weeks to decide, if you want, but we'd like for you to make a decision and stick with it for at least the school year. If you stay with me, we'll have to figure out who's going to stay with you or who you'll stay with when I'm on road trips, but that is something we can tackle when the time comes."

"I-I don't know what to say," she says.

"You don't have to say anything right now. I know this is a lot to take in all at once, but we wanted to let you start thinking about it as soon as possible. I felt really bad about your dad just now moving here and me needing to move, and that's where this idea was born. While I'll miss you every second we're apart, I'll also support you if you decide to stay here. I know this is the only place you've called home, where all your friends are, school, your whole life."

"I can think about it for a little bit?" she asks, looking between the two of us.

"Absolutely. I have to start packing up and be in Texas in just a few weeks, but you can take a few weeks and decide. Spend time with your dad, maybe make a trip down to Texas once I get a place and you can come to check it out, if you want," Michelle tells her.

"Okay," Ellie says, blowing out a big breath. "Any other surprises, or are we done for the day?"

"That's all for today." I chuckle with her as I calm her nerves that we're not going to drop any other bombs in her lap.

Our food comes and, with it, some pleasant conversation. We don't bring up Michelle's job, or the decision that Ellie needs to make in the coming weeks. She's a big girl and can make it on her own.

CHAPTER 2

Avery

I STARE at my computer screen, the numbers running together in a jumbled mess. "What the hell am I even looking at?" I mumble under my breath as I try and make sense of what a client sent me. My puppy, Max, comes over and nudges me with his wet nose, pulling my attention from my computer.

"Is it time for a walk?" I ask him as I scratch the top of his head. His ears perk up at the word walk. He loves going outside and quickly learned the word. "All right, buddy, we'll go," I tell him as he tries to jump up into my lap excitedly. The silly boy thinks he's a lap dog, not a large, seventy-pound Goldendoodle.

I stand up from my desk, stretching out the kinks in my neck and back that I get when sitting at the computer for hours upon hours each day. A quick pit stop in the bathroom, and I'm ready to slip on some sandals and make our way outside and into the sunshine.

Max and I take our time, leisurely walking around the block. We stop in the little park two blocks over to let him chase the ball for a few minutes. They added the fenced dog area last summer, and it has become a very convenient place for us to go when Max needs to get some energy out. "Okay, boy, it's time to head back home," I tell him when he brings the ball back to me. I reclip his leash before we head out of the fenced area and onto the path that will take us back home.

Max and I take the stairs up the one flight to my condo door rather than the elevator, as most people do. "Did you have a good time?" I ask him as we approach the top step. "You were such a good boy today," I praise him.

We enter the hallway, and my front door is just down a little bit. As we pass my neighbor's door, it swings open and a large man steps out, followed by another man, not nearly as large as the first. He's also trailed by a young girl—probably in her teens, if I had to guess.

"Oh, sorry," I tell the first man as Max tries to jump on him, licking him.

"No problem; what kind of dog is he?" the man asks, and the timbre of his voice does things to me. Things I can't even express with words.

It takes me a second to register his question and

sputter my answer. "He's a Goldendoodle. Max is still just a puppy, even though he doesn't quite look like it based on his size." I chuckle nervously.

"You're a good boy, aren't you, Max?" The man coos at him as he gives him a good pat down.

"Aww, Dad, he's so cute. Can we get a dog?" the girl asks the man as she moves to be next to him and close enough to give Max some belly rubs.

"We'll talk about it, but I make no promises," he tells her. I have to wonder if that was to appease her, for now, or if he'll consider getting her a dog.

"Are you looking at the unit for sale?" I ask.

"We are," the man says, and my belly flops at the thought of him living just a few walls away from me. "I'm Ryker, and this is my daughter, Ellie." He introduces the two of them and holds a hand out for me to shake.

"Nice meeting you, I'm Avery."

"It is very nice to meet you, Avery. Can I ask your opinions about this place? I need somewhere safe, especially since I have a daughter to be thinking about," he says.

"It's great. I've been here for a couple of years and have never had an issue. It's safe, not super noisy; everyone I've encountered has been super nice."

"That's great to hear. We liked the unit," he says before turning to the other man with him.

"Let's write up an offer. Full price, cash, close in ten days. Only subject to an inspection," he rattles off to the man, who quickly types everything out on his phone.

"Of course. I'll get it drawn up as soon as I'm back at the office and sent to the seller's agent."

"Nice meeting you, Avery; looks like we might be neighbors, so we'll possibly see you around," Ryker says before he follows his realtor and daughter out the door I came in.

"It was nice meeting you," I call at their retreating backs. "Let's get you home and have some water," I say to Max. He stands back up and quickly makes his way to my door, where he patiently waits for me to unlock and open it. As soon as it opens, he heads straight for the water bowl, emptying it in minutes.

I sit back down at my computer, the numbers on the screen are still a jumbled mess as I try to decipher what is going on with this report.

It took me an hour, but I finally made some headway, fixing the central issue for my client.

I genuinely love my job, especially the flexibility working from home brings me. It's a little isolating, at times, but I also like working in my pj's, if I feel like it.

A knock on my door pulls my attention and wakes Max up. He runs for the door, barking as if he doesn't just want to lick the person on the other side to death rather than be a mean and protective dog. I swear, he's never met a stranger in his life. He's just a big fluffy ball of love.

I peek out the peephole and see my neighbor standing in the hall.

"Max, sit," I instruct, giving him the sign we learned in his training class. Even if his tail is still moving a mile a minute with excitement, he does as told. I unlock and pull the door open. "Hello, Ruth," I greet the older woman who's lived next door to me for the past few years.

"Hi, Avery, how are you?" she asks, and reaches her hand out for Max to sniff before she scratches the top of his head.

"I'm good, thanks for asking. How are you?"

"Wonderful. I just got a call with an offer for my unit. Full asking price!" she tells me excitedly.

"How wonderful. I think I might have met the buyer when I returned from a walk with Max," I tell her. "He seemed nice, had a teenage daughter with him," I tell her.

"Oh, that's just lovely. He must need something quickly, as they want to close in just ten days. I don't know if I can get my things moved so quickly," she goes on to tell me.

"If you need help finding movers, I don't mind doing some calling for you," I offer.

"So very kind of you, and I might take you up on your offer. I might have to pay to put my things in storage for a few months."

"What were your plans for everything?" I ask.

"I figured I'd have more time. I was going to

try and sell as much as I could that I won't need before moving into my son's house, but I just don't see being able to do so in the next ten days."

"Can he come and help you at all? I can set aside some time this week to help you in the evenings. You could have an estate-like sale this weekend and see how much you can sell off, and then go from there on what you are willing to donate versus what you'll need to store."

"That's a great idea." She mulls it over. "And you're sure you don't mind helping me out?" she asks.

"Not at all. I didn't have anything going on this weekend, so it will give me something to do."

"All right, I'll go to the store, get some tags, and start going through things. It's all just happening so fast!"

"Have you already accepted the offer?" I ask. "Maybe you can have your realtor counter back that you need a little bit more time, even if you push it to twenty or thirty days?" I suggest.

"I hadn't considered that. I didn't want to upset the buyer since it was an all-cash offer. You don't get those all too often."

I try to think back to the man I met in the hallway, Ryker, I believe he said his name was. I didn't take him as being some rich asshole, so while he might need a place quickly, it wouldn't surprise me, either, if he's easy to work with. I got good vibes from him, the little we interacted.

"It doesn't hurt to ask. The worst thing that happens is they say no and keep the offer as is."

"You are so full of help today. I'm sure going to miss having you right next door."

"I'll miss you, too, Ruth. Who else am I going to bring my stress-baked goods to?"

"Maybe the new man next door?" she suggests, bouncing her eyebrows at me. "Maybe he'll be single and looking to mingle."

I can't help but chuckle at Ruth's words. She's always telling me how I need to get out more and date. She's tried setting me up with so many random men. The delivery guy from her favorite Italian restaurant, the FedEx driver, her son's best friend. If she even thinks a guy is relatively—and I do mean relatively—my age and single, she tries to send him my way. "Maybe, but he did have a daughter, so don't hold your breath over him being single."

"Single dads are supposed to be chick magnets," Ruth says, matter of factly.

"You are a hoot, you know that?" I tell her, laughing once again at the words coming out of her mouth.

"Someone around here has to keep things interesting," she says, primping her hair as only an old lady can.

"All right, I should probably get back to work. I

can come over in a little while and help you start marking things for sale, maybe take a few pictures of items, and make some posts about the sale on social media to start getting the word out."

"I'll order us some dinner, how does that sound?" she offers.

"Like a plan. I'll finish work, take Max out, and then be over about six."

"See you then!" she says before turning on her heel and heading down the hall.

I close my door, locking it, before leaning against it and blowing out a big breath. Ruth is a lovely older woman who has become a good friend over the years. I'll miss her when she moves in with her son. I'm glad she's moving in with him, as she's had some health issues the past year and sometimes needs a little extra help from time to time. I like knowing she'll have someone right there all the time to look after her.

CHAPTER 3
Ryker

"DAD," Ellie calls out from the small bedroom.

"Yeah?" I answer as I set the weights down I was using. I've got a small area in the corner of the living room set up with a yoga mat, free weights, and a jump rope; just a few items I need to work out on days I don't go hit up the gym.

"Can we go shopping for furniture today?" she asks.

"I suppose. Did you have somewhere in mind?"

"Not really. I figured just one of the large furniture stores that carry things for every room."

"Okay, let me grab a quick shower, and then we can go look."

I step into the bathroom and turn the water on. While it heats up, I strip out of my tank top and shorts. The spray of water feels good on my muscles. The bed in this rental has been an adjustment my body hasn't taken kindly to. I'm definitely looking forward to getting into my new condo and having my bed delivered. I didn't keep much from my place in Indianapolis; most of it was cheap, pieced-together items. I never bought a place to call home. I just always rented and furnished my places with the bare necessities. With me now calling California home, and having my daughter living with me full-time, I need to make this place home.

I'm still coming to terms with the idea she decided to stay with me. I was convinced Ellie would want to move with her mom to Texas. But in true teenage girl fashion, she shocked both of us when she decided to stay here with me. I think her decision hurt Michelle, but we both agreed to support her in whatever decision she made. We all agreed she'd need to stick to her decision for at least the school year, as we don't want her bouncing around mid-school year and getting behind on her studies.

"I'm ready when you are," I call out as I pull a T-shirt over my head. I rub my towel over my hair to help soak up some of the water before quickly running a comb through it.

"I'm ready!" Ellie squeals as she comes rushing out of her room. "Can I pick out an entire bedroom set?" she asks.

"You can pick out whatever you want," I tell her honestly. "I want you to decorate it however you want. We can paint and put up posters or pictures.

Whatever you want, Ellie Bean." I pull her into a side hug.

"I'm so excited. When do we get to move in to the new place?" she asks.

"Another five days. The seller asked for a little more time than I'd originally put in my offer, and I agreed. I have the lease on this place through the end of August, so I didn't mind giving her some more time."

"Are we moving in right away?" she asks.

"I figured once I have the keys, I can see the condition for paint and carpet. Sometimes you don't notice how bad those things are until everything is out. I'm sure a fresh coat of paint will be needed, and replacing flooring is much easier to do when the place is empty. So, now's the time to do all of that."

"So, a few weeks, then, until we move in?" she asks.

"Probably," I say as we get into my car. I pull up the GPS on my phone, look up the nearest furniture store, and hit go.

"Dad, look!" Ellie says, taking off for a bedroom display with "teenage girl" written all over it.

"Looks nice," I state as I stop by the display. I look over the information on it as she checks out each piece they have set up.

"Can I get this one?" she asks.

"Let's look around and make sure you don't like anything else," I suggest.

"Okay," she quickly agrees and hops off the bed. I follow her around the store as she oohs and aahs over different displays. "Can we go check out another store before we decide?" she asks once we've looked at every display.

"If that's what you'd like. Do you not like the first one anymore?" I ask.

"I do, but I don't want to pick it if I like something else better."

"You'll have to make up your mind, Ellie Bean." I chuckle at her indecisiveness.

"I know, but it's not like I can get new stuff all the time. This will have to last me for the next few years."

"I suppose." I drape an arm over her shoulder as we walk through the store. "How about some lunch, first. Your old man is hungry."

"Dad, you aren't old," she tells me, poking me in the ribs.

"At least someone thinks so."

"Dad, you're, like, thirty-five. That isn't old."

"I feel like I'm fifty, some days."

"Well, that's because you get slammed into the boards regularly."

"Hey, now, I do some of the slamming," I protest.

"I'm sure you do," she laughs at me.

"Are you excited about me playing here, now?" I ask once we're back in the car.

"Yeah, it's still hard to believe that this is all happening," she admits, and I feel the same way.

"I'm sure it will be an adjustment for all of us. If you change your mind before the summer is up, just say the word, and I'll put you on a flight to your mom."

"Trying to get rid of me already?" she teases. I flash her a smirk. She knows better than to believe that nonsense.

"Never," I tell her.

"Do you know how much my popularity will shoot up when people realize my dad is one of the Shockwaves?" she asks.

"Is that all I'm good for, now? Getting you popularity points at school? I see where I rank."

"That's not what I meant." She laughs and smacks my arm.

"Sure, it isn't," I tease. "It's okay, Ellie Bean. You can use me for my status." I flash her a quick wink so she knows I'm just messing with her.

"What's going to happen when you go on road trips?" she asks. When Michelle and I sat down and laid out everything for her, we brought this up but said we'd have to figure it out later.

"I feel kind of weird hiring a nanny. You're fifteen, not five, but I also can't leave town and not have someone watching you. Your mom suggested you stay with a friend from school, which might work for some shorter trips, but that's a lot to ask of a friend's parents. What are your thoughts?" I ask.

"I like the idea of staying with a friend, most likely Steph, but I don't think it will work every time."

"We'll figure it out. We've got time. Maybe one of the other guys will have a girlfriend or wife willing to stay with you or have you stay with them. Some of them are pretty young."

"Maybe," she agrees.

"Where do you want to get lunch?" I ask.

"Can we get sushi?" she asks.

"Sure, where from?" I ask. She pulls up a place on her phone and directs me to the restaurant.

CHAPTER 4

Avery

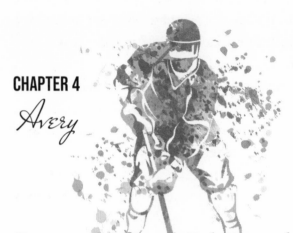

"I PROMISE to stay in touch, Ruth," I assure her as she stands in front of my door. The final load of her belongings was taken down to the moving truck just a few minutes ago. I've helped her sort through all her belongings, sell what she could, donate others, and pack what was going with her to her son's place.

"You'd better, dear. I want to hear all about the hunky new owner. Maybe you should bake some of your cookies this weekend to take him as a welcome gift," she suggests.

"I'll think about it," I tell her. "I'll call you some-time next week to check-in and make sure you've settled in."

"Oh goody, you can update me on the hunk then," she giddily says, clapping her wrinkly hands together as if she's a little schoolgirl.

I pull Ruth into a hug. As crazy as she makes me,

I'm going to miss having her next door. She was the extra grandmother I never knew I needed. "Take care of yourself but try not to drive your son crazy with your antics," I tell her as I squeeze her, not too tight to hurt her.

"Of course, I'll take care of myself, and if I don't drive him crazy, who will?" she asks.

"Oh, Ruth. Don't ever change," I tell her as I release her from our embrace.

"Never! And don't think I'll forget about you updating me on the hunky new neighbor. I expect a full report on him and his marital status."

"Aye, Aye, captain." I salute Ruth. I watch as she makes her way down the hall and to the elevator. I wipe quickly at the tear escaping my eyes. I never realized how much Ruth moving would affect me, but here I am, standing at my door, crying over a neighbor moving across town. How pathetic.

Max nudges my hand with his head. He's very aware of my mood and knows just when I need some cheering up. He continues to nudge me as I lazily scratch the top of his head. He gets my attention when he leaves my side, only to return with the leash in his mouth. "Okay, buddy, I get the hint, you want to go for a walk."

I grab a pair of socks and slip my tennis shoes on. I refill my water bottle before clipping the leash to his collar, and we head out the door. The sun is shining bright today and feels fantastic on my face as we walk down to the park. Max is crazy excited when we arrive as the dog park is filled with dogs of all sizes. Once inside the gate, I unclip him and watch as he takes off for the other side of the fenced in area, finding dog friends along the way to chase and play with.

I wave to a few people I recognize as regulars as I make my way to the far side of the park, where an open bench sits. Max comes to find me, always observant of where I am when we're here. He's protective in his own ways, and I wouldn't change it for anything. I researched for months before I decided to get a dog. The early days were hectic, but I couldn't imagine my life without him, now.

I'M RELAXING on the couch, some music playing low in the background as I read my newest Kaylee Ryan book.

Max starts barking, obviously hearing something outside, the way he's looking at the door.

"Settle," I tell him, and he looks back at me but doesn't move from his place at the door. "What's got your attention so focused?" I ask him as I set my kindle down and make my way to the door. I can hear muffled voices in the hall, so I peek out the peephole and see a few people waiting outside

Ruth's old door. My new neighbor must be moving in, from the looks of it. He's not wasting any time, considering how Ruth just left this morning.

I like her idea of welcoming him and his family to the building with some baked goods, so I turn for the kitchen. I pull everything out for my famous chocolate chip caramel bars. I have friends who will call and specifically request I bring these when we get together. They've become my signature dessert and, thankfully, are super easy to make.

I clean up the mess I made with my bars in the oven, then start the dishwasher. While the bars bake, I head for my bathroom and take a quick shower. Between the sweaty trip to the park earlier and not showering this morning, I need one before taking the bars next door.

I wrap a fluffy towel around my body before wrapping up my hair. I grab my favorite bottle of lotion and take it to my bed. I slather every inch of skin, trying my best to keep it well hydrated and in the best condition. I don't have a vain bone in my body, but I'd still like to keep myself from wrinkling before I'm thirty.

Once I'm well moisturized, I head for my closet. I stare at everything, wondering what I should wear to take baked goods to my new neighbor. From what I remember of our one encounter, he was gorgeous. However, I don't want to come off as a hussy, especially if he is married or has a girlfriend. I don't need my new neighbors to hate me from their first day next door. I finally decide on shorts; they hit me mid-thigh, so nothing too scandalous, and a flowy tank top. Everything necessary is covered, yet it is flattering on me.

With my outfit picked, I head back into the bathroom and comb through my hair. I have to stop for a couple of minutes when the timer on my phone starts going off, alerting me it's time to take the bars out of the oven to let them cool off.

I pull out my hairdryer and flat iron. Once my hair is dry, I start adding curls with my flat iron. I don't usually take the time to get all made up, especially to go next door, but I'm enjoying myself tonight. I can't explain why I want to look my best, but I do.

I give myself a once-over in the mirror with a little bit of mascara and lip gloss added to my face. I don't look overdone, but well pulled together. I hope I don't come off as someone who's trying too hard.

The bars are still a little on the warm side, so I pop them into the freezer to help cool them enough so I can cut and plate them. I plop down on the couch again, and Max jumps up to lay down next to me with his head firmly in my lap. "Who's a good boy?" I ask him as I scratch his ears. His ears perk up, and he looks like he's in heaven as I scratch away. I read a few chapters before checking on the bars once again. They're finally cooled enough for me to cut them and arrange them on the plate I have to take next door.

I kiss the top of Max's head before leaving. I stand outside my neighbor's door and suck in a calming breath before raising my hand to knock on the frame. Before my knuckles hit the wood, the door flies open and the girl I saw a few weeks ago stands at the door.

"Oh, hi!" she squeaks in surprise.

"Hi, I'm Avery. I live next door and want to welcome your family to the building," I tell her as I hold the plate filled with the chocolate-caramel goodness.

"Thank you. Hey, Dad, come here," she says, calling for him over her shoulder.

I look into the unit, waiting for Ryker to come into my view. The moment he does, it feels like the air in the room is sucked out. He's gorgeous in that rugged, man-next-door way. Whatever this man does must be physical because his body is all sinewy muscles from what I can see and how his clothes hug him. My center clenches in need. I've never had this kind of visceral reaction to a man, especially one I've hardly had a conversation with.

"Avery brought us a welcome gift," the girl tells him as he comes to stand next to his daughter.

"That's very thoughtful of you, thank you," he says, reaching out to take the plate from my hands. His fingers graze mine in the transfer, and electrical currents run up them at his touch. If just a brush of his fingers against my own creates such a strong reaction, I can only imagine what him touching me elsewhere would be like.

I realize he's said something to me, and I've yet to answer. I shake my head, getting my mind out of the gutter, where it has so clearly gone. "You're welcome. I love to bake, but then am left with being the only one to eat what I make, so I used to bring it over to Ruth, but now she's gone, and you're here," I tell him as I ramble on. "So, tell me now if you don't like random baked goods showing up."

"I love baked good," the girl pipes up. "I'm Ellie," she tells me.

"It's nice to meet you, Ellie. Your name is so pretty, I love it."

"Thanks," she says, giving me a small smile. "Holy crap, these are amazing," she says around a mouthful of a cookie bar.

"They're one of my most requested items from my friends and family," I tell her as she devours the rest of the bar in her hand.

"I can see why. It was delicious and addicting."

I laugh lightly at her comment. "I've heard that before, as well."

"Let me try one of these things, then," Ryker says as he grabs one from the platter. My eyes are glued to his face as I watch him take his first bite. His eyes pop open with his first bite, and I can tell he's enjoying it just as much as Ellie did. "This is incredible, even if I will be paying for it at the gym tomorrow."

The idea of Ryker at the gym has so many mental pictures going through my mind.

"Would you like to come in?" he finally asks. Things turn a little awkward as I stand in his open doorway.

"I don't want to impose. I just wanted to say welcome and let you know I'm almost always around as I work from home, so don't hesitate to knock on my door if you need something."

"Thanks, I'll keep that in mind," he says. "We are just here making a list of things we want to be updated or fixed before moving in."

"What a smart idea. Are you planning on any major changes?" I ask.

"No, just some fresh paint and flooring. I also plan on putting in new appliances. The painter and flooring guys just left. They needed to measure so they know how much material to buy."

"Oh, wow, some big changes coming."

"I figured now is the time to make any changes we might want. Not having furniture in here yet will make changing things so much easier."

"That makes sense. When do you think you'll be moving in?"

"Hopefully, it doesn't take too long. I've already got the painters set up to start Monday."

"Sounds like a good plan."

"Have you lived here long?" he asks.

"I bought the place about two years ago, so I'm your woman if you need any recommendations for restaurants around here," I offer.

"Good to know. I'm just moving to town, and Ellie will be living with me instead of with her mom," he tells me.

"Where did you move from?" I ask, and their situation piques my interest.

"That's a complicated answer, but I was most recently in Indianapolis."

"My dad's a professional hockey player. The new San Francisco team selected him," Ellie interjects.

"Oh, wow. I have a co-worker who's been going on and on about the new team. He's going to freak out if I ever tell him my new neighbor is one of the players."

"If you ever need some tickets, I'm your man," Ryker says.

"Thanks for the offer. I probably won't ever tell him you live next door, otherwise, he'll never stop bugging me about you."

"I understand. I try and keep a low profile, so I appreciate you not telling everyone my business."

"I can't imagine what I'd tell anyone about you, but I'll try and keep from spreading rumors around."

"I appreciate it, especially now that Ellie will be living with me full-time. I need my daughter to be safe."

"Of course," I tell him, knowing I don't talk to many people, so his secret is safe with me. "I should get out of your hair. I just wanted to welcome you to the building and bring you the cookie bars. If you need anything, I'm right next door," I tell him before stepping back to the door.

"Thanks again, and I'm sure we'll see you around. I apologize in advance if there's some excessive noise coming from my condo while the work is being done. It will hopefully only be for a week or so."

"If it's super loud, I can just put in my earbuds and listen to music or my book while I work."

"I'll remind them you're working next door and to keep things to a minimum."

"Sounds good. I'll see you around," I tell them before heading back to my condo.

CHAPTER 5

Ryker

MOVING DAY HAS FINALLY ARRIVED. Once Ellie picked out the bedroom set she wanted, and I finalized the living room furniture and my bedroom furniture, I had it all set up to be delivered today. This way, we can move everything into the new condo in one day.

"Ellie Bean," I call out to her from the living room.

"Yeah, Dad?" she calls back.

"I was going to make a run to Target. Did you want to come?" I ask. Since my summer rental was fully furnished, I need basic staples like trash cans, rugs, towels, pots, and pans. It's like setting up a house for the first time all over again.

"Yeah, give me five minutes, and I'll be ready," she says.

I take the time to start a list on my phone, so we hopefully don't forget anything we need tonight. I'm sure we'll be back at the store tomorrow for something we think of.

"I'm ready. I need a few things for my room," she tells me, so I grab my keys and we head out the door.

I grab a cart after we enter, and we head for the home section. We load the cart up with kitchen items, trash cans, sheets, towels, and so much stuff, Ellie has to go back up to the front of the store and grab a second cart.

"I don't think we can fit anything else in these carts, Dad," Ellie comments as we push our full carts toward the checkout.

"If we forgot it, we can come back for it tomorrow. I'm exhausted and need some dinner. What are you feeling like tonight?"

"How about pizza?" she suggests.

"If you want pizza, we can do pizza," I tell her.

We check out at the store and very carefully get our overfilled carts to my car. Once it is fully loaded, we head toward home.

"What kind of pizza do you want?" I ask as we wait at a red light.

Ellie finishes off her Starbucks drink she grabbed before we left Target. "I'm good with just about anything. Pepperoni, meat lovers, cheese, whatever you want, just no mushrooms or olives," she reminds me, like I don't know she hates both of those things.

"You got it," I tell her as the light turns green.

Once we're back to the condo and parked, I pull

my phone out and find a local pizza place that offers delivery. I quickly place our order before emptying all our bags from the car and getting them upstairs. Ellie jumps right in, helping me unpack everything and figure out where it will go. All the kitchen items get loaded into the dishwasher to be cleaned.

"Thanks for your help, kiddo," I tell Ellie as I pull her into a side hug. She's always been a great kid, but moments like these remind me just how good she actually is.

"When will the food be here?" Ellie asks.

I pull my phone out of my pocket and tap the screen to life, opening the app from the pizza place. "App shows our order has left their nearest location and is on the way here."

"Oh good, I'm starving," she tells me.

"Same," I agree with her.

"Once I get my room set up, can Steph come for a sleepover?" she asks.

"I don't see why not. Heck, if you wanted to, we could work together to get things set up and you can see if she can come tonight," I offer.

"She's busy tonight, but I'll see if she can come tomorrow," Ellie says before she bounds down the hall to her room. I continue putting things away in the kitchen until my phone rings from the security door downstairs.

I open the door after the delivery guy knocks.

"Two pizzas, an order of wings, and a dessert cookie," he rattles off our order.

"Sounds about right," I tell him as I accept the stack of boxes and hand over a cash tip.

"Thanks, have a great night," he says as he pockets the ten I gave him.

"You too," I call at his retreating back. "Ellie Bean, dinner's here," I call out loudly, so she hopefully hears me in her room. She loves to listen to music, so she doesn't always hear when she's called for. "That was fast." I chuckle as she comes running.

"I told you I was starving," she says as she grabs a plate and starts dishing up from the boxes. We sit at the bar, as it's the only place with an easy-to-clean-off spot. Moving is always a pain in the ass, but add needing to furnish a home fully, and this place is a mess.

"Is there anything you want to do before school starts next month?" I ask as we both slow down on our eating.

"Can we go on a trip?" she asks.

"Where are you thinking?" I ask.

"I don't know. I just want to go somewhere and do something fun."

"I'll make you a deal, you pick the place and a few fun things to do, and we'll go do it. If you want to see if Steph can come, invite her along."

"Really?" she asks, perking up at the idea.

"Absolutely," I confirm. "It can be anywhere. My

stipulations are you plan the trip. I'll help with transportation and lodging, if you need it, but otherwise, it's all up to you and Steph."

"Thank you, Dad!" Ellie giddily thanks me as she claps her hands together, her excitement pouring off her.

"Don't make me regret this offer." I full-on belly laugh at her excitement.

"Never," she tells me, turning serious as she does. "I'm going to go text Steph and start looking places up." She stands from the bar and takes her plate to the sink before disappearing back down the hall and into her room.

CHAPTER 6
Avery

MAX POPS up from his nap on the couch and lets out a bark at the knock on the door. It shocks me slightly as I wasn't expecting anyone, especially anyone with the code to unlock the door downstairs. I look through the peephole and see my new sexy neighbor standing on the other side. "Max, stay," I instruct, and he does as he's told.

I open the door and find Ryker on the other side, his hands shoved into the pockets of his jeans. The Shockwaves T-shirt he has on pulls across his muscular chest, and I find myself daydreaming about what he'd look like *without* the T-shirt on. "Hi," I finally greet him.

"Hey, Avery. How's it going?" he asks.

"Oh good, and you? Are you fully moved in, now?"

"Yeah, I think so," he says.

He grips the back of his neck, and I can't miss the way his muscles flex as he does so. What I wouldn't give to lick some of those muscles. I shake my head, trying to get rid of those thoughts about my neighbor. I know very little about him and have no right to be thinking about him naked.

"That's good, moving always sucks."

"Yeah," he agrees with a chuckle. "I was just stopping by to ask a favor. We're going out of town for a week. Can you just keep an eye out for anything out of order with my place? I don't think I'll have any packages delivered, but just in case I do, can you grab them?"

"Sure, do you need anything watered or fed while gone?" I ask.

"Nope, I'm taking Ellie with me. She actually planned the trip," he says.

"Oh, how fun! Where are you headed?" I ask.

"Florida. We're going to Universal and Disney for a couple of days before getting on a cruise for another few nights."

"Sounds amazing," I tell him. "She must be a great planner if she picked all of that."

"I think Dad's unlimited credit card had some help." He chuckles.

"Well, yeah, if someone gave me their credit card and said to plan a trip, no budget, I'd do some damage for sure," I tell him.

"Oh yeah, where would you go?" he asks, and leans against the doorframe.

"I have a few bucket list places; London, , O, the Maldives, just to name a few."

"All great places," he says.

"Have you been?" I ask.

"London and the Maldives, but never Spain."

"So jealous," I say, blowing out a huge breath. "Unless I win the lottery, I don't foresee myself ever making it to those places, unfortunately."

"London isn't all that bad to get to. Just got to watch for cheap flights," he says.

"I'm sure I could pull London off, but my true top of the bucket list is the Maldives. I'll mock up a trip every few months and get depressed when I see the total, especially when I don't have anyone to go with me. It seems like more of a place you'd go with a significant other, not your best friend or by yourself."

"Yeah, I went to a buddy's wedding there. It was a gorgeous place, but I agree, I'd want it to be with someone special to share it with, if I ever went back. It has a very romantic atmosphere."

"I can't remember if you said yes or no to having any plants that will need watering?" I ask, bringing the conversation back to where it was.

"Nope, but I could get you a key to have, just in case. Then, if anything is delivered, you can put it inside the door and not have to store it for me until I'm back."

"Either works, I don't mind," I tell him, not wanting him to feel like he has to give me a key to his place.

"I appreciate it, and as I said, I don't think you'll need to do anything, but just in case, I like knowing someone is around who can help, if needed."

"Have a great time. Is it just you and Ellie going?" I ask.

"Her best friend, Steph, is also joining us, so please say a prayer for me that two teenage girls don't kill me in the middle of the trip," he says, laughing again.

"God speed," I tell him, doing my best to hold in my laughter.

"I'll need it and every ounce of my sanity. I thought traveling with twenty-some-odd broody hockey players all over the country was bad, but something tells me traveling with two teenage girls has nothing on the rowdy bunch I'm used to."

"Probably not," I agree with him.

"I can give you my number, that way you can call or text if something is wrong."

"Sure, let me grab my cell, quick. Do you want to come in while I grab it? Max is going crazy on the couch and would like to come say hi."

"Of course." Ryker follows me into my unit and closes the door behind him. I signal to Max that he can get down off the couch and he bolts for the front door and where Ryker is standing. I watch as he leans down and pets him, Max loving the undivided attention he's receiving right now. I grab my cell and unlock it so I can open the contacts and add Ryker in.

"I'm ready for it now," I tell Ryker, prepared to type in the numbers he rattles off. "Got you saved, and your phone should chime any second now with an incoming text from me, so you'll have my number, as well."

"Thanks, I truly do appreciate it."

"Anytime. I'm a huge homebody. If it wasn't for Max and his need to go outside multiple times each day, I might go days before I step outside."

"I should get going. We have to leave for the airport in the next half hour or so," he tells me before standing from where he was sitting on his haunches, petting Max.

"Have a great time, take lots of pictures," I tell him.

"Will do, and maybe, once I get back, I can give you a little tour of my place now that it's been renovated."

"I'd love that. I love watching how small things can change the entire feeling and flow of a room."

"So, Dear, how's the hunky new neighbor?" Ruth asks as we sit across from one another at a local coffee shop.

"He's nice and he's got the sweetest daughter."

"Oh, how nice," she says before taking a drink of her iced tea. "Married?" she asks.

"Nope, he is single," I tell her, winking, since I know that will be her next question.

"Good, good. We're making progress, it sounds."

"I don't know if I'd call it progress, I've only talked to him a couple of times, but he's seemed nice when I have. He's on a trip right now with his daughter," I tell her. "He came over this morning and asked if I could keep an eye out for anything out of place or for packages."

"Interesting," she muses as she takes another sip.

"Just neighborly," I tell her. "Not much different than I'd do for you or you did for me," I remind her.

"I suppose you're right," she agrees.

"How are you settling in?" I ask.

"Oh fine, even if I feel like I'm being hovered over, now. I never have a moment to myself, it seems."

"I'm sure it isn't that bad." I chuckle at how Ruth over exaggerates her current situation.

"Feels like I'm a teenager again, sneaking around, so I don't get busted out past curfew."

"Really, Ruth?" I question, raising an eyebrow in question.

"Well, you know what I mean. You go from living on your own with no one to question or judge you, to living under someone else's roof, and your life will change."

"I still don't think it would be that bad. Don't you enjoy being around family more?" I ask, bringing the positives to the forefront.

"I do, but it's just an adjustment period."

"It certainly is, but I'm sure it will feel like normal shortly."

"I hope you're right," she tells me.

CHAPTER 7
Ryker

"Dad!" Ellie squeals when she sees our boarding passes and notices I booked us in first class.

"What?" I play dumb.

"First class?" she questions, making sure she's looking at the information correctly.

"Yep. Figured if we're flying across the country, we might as well be comfortable."

"You're the best!" she tells me as she and Steph freak out together.

"Thanks again, Mr. Jorgensen, for inviting me along," Steph tells me.

"You're welcome, but please don't call me Mr. Jorgensen. It makes me think my dad is here. Ryker is fine," I tell her.

"Will do, Ryker," she says.

We make our way through the airport and to the

gate. Our first-class seats came with an express line to get through security.

"Can we go get something to eat before we board?" Ellie asks.

"I suppose. You'll also be fed on the flight since we're first class," I tell them.

"We'll just grab a quick snack, then. Do you want anything?" she asks.

"Where are you going?"

The girls look at one another, and I swear they can talk through facial clues as they don't speak a word before turning my way and answering at the same time, "Starbucks." At their same answer, they break into a fit of giggles, and I'm once again finding myself wondering how I'm going to survive this trip with two teenage girls all by myself.

"Get me a tall coffee with cream," I tell Ellie as I dig my wallet out and hand her some cash.

"Thanks, Dad. You're the best," she says, and kisses my cheek before the girls turn around and head to the Starbucks I can see from my seat. I watch them closely, making sure they don't need my help.

"HOLY CRAP, THIS PLACE IS HUGE," Steph tells Ellie as we walk into the suite I rented.

"Yeah, it is," she replies. "We could practically get lost in here."

"I don't think it's *that* big," I say from behind them. "Will this do for you two this week?" I ask as I lean against the doorjamb.

"Oh yes," Ellie says.

"This is going to be the most epic week ever," Steph says.

"I'm glad the two of you think so." I head back the way I came, finding the main bedroom easily. I set my suitcase down and get to unpacking it. I'm one of the strange people who unpack when at a hotel. There's just something about being able to put your suitcase away for the bulk of a trip. I even do this when on road trips during the season.

I WAKE up to the sound of my phone ringing. I wipe my face with one hand as I fish for the phone with my other. My eyes focus on the name flashing, *Avery*.

"Hello," I say, the sleepiness evident in my voice.

"Hi, Ryker, it's Avery. I'm so sorry to bother you, especially at this hour. There's been a minor emergency."

"Shit, what's up?"

"The unit above yours had a pipe burst, and water was pouring in. It has stopped now, but it did get in and cause some damage. I've taken a look, myself, and you'll need some new flooring and possibly some drywall replaced. I got as much cleaned up as I could, but you might need to call in a company when you get back to make sure mold doesn't start growing due to any missed water."

"Fuck," I say under my breath. I scrub my face, trying like hell to wake up.

"I'm sorry," Avery whispers.

"Nothing to be sorry for. Thanks for calling and for taking care of things for me. I owe you. I'll give my insurance company a call tomorrow and see how they want me to proceed."

"Probably a good place to start," she says. "If there's anything you need me to do, I'm just a phone call away."

"Thanks. I'll see how much I can do while away, but I might take you up on it if I can get a company lined up for tomorrow or the next day and need someone to let them in."

"Of course, just let me know."

"Thanks for the call. I'll keep you in the loop once I know anything."

"Night, Ryker." Avery's sweet voice soothes me before she disconnects the call. My mind drifts to what other words I could make fall from those lips if she was in bed with me. It wanders to the uncharted territory when it comes to the beautiful Avery, my body revs up, ready to show her a good time.

My cock swells as I imagine backing her up against the wall, claiming her lips with my own before I'd carry her to my bed. It wouldn't take me long to strip her clothes off so I could bury my head between her legs and make her cry out in pleasure as I make her come on my tongue. Or maybe I'd lie on the bed and let her sit on my face, giving her all the control over her orgasm. "Fuck," I groan as I grip my cock. The slideshow on display in my mind is not helping the situation below the sheet. I imagine her hand wrapped around my shaft as I stroke myself. How she'd wrap her lips around the tip, licking and sucking as she teases me until I come.

I fling the sheet off of me, my body warming up as I near my release. It only takes a few more strokes before I'm releasing all over my abs. My breathing is labored as I lay here, exhausted from the late-night hour, exhausted from the day we had, exhausted from the moment I just had thinking of Avery.

CHAPTER 8

Avery

A LOUD KNOCK on my door startles me. I wasn't expecting anyone, so I quietly make my way to the door. I check the peephole and see Ryker standing on the other side of the door.

I quickly pull it open, schooling my features so I don't fawn all over him. I take in his appearance, T-shirt pulled tight over his muscles, jeans that hug his body like they were cut specifically to fit his frame. His hands are tucked into the pockets of his jeans in a casual stance.

"Hey, you're back," I greet.

"Yeah, just got here about twenty minutes ago. Thought I should let you know."

"How was the trip?" I ask.

"We had a great time," he confirms, a smile pulling at the corners of his lips. He has such a great smile, and I make it my mission to see him do so as much as possible.

"That's great to hear! Did the girls drive you crazy?" I ask.

"Not too bad. They pretty much kept each other occupied, so it worked out in my favor to have Ellie bring a friend with her."

"Makes sense," I muse. "Have you checked out the damage yet?"

"Yeah," he says, bringing a hand up to the back of his neck. The movement causes his bicep to flex, and I swear the movement sends a bolt of electricity directly to my core. How—*how*—is that a sexy movement? "The contractor will be here in the morning to give me a quote for fixing everything. I'm hoping they can start ASAP, and get it done quickly."

"Is your insurance going to pay for it?" I ask.

"Yes, I just have to cover my deductible."

"Well, that's a plus," I tell him.

"I guess," he agrees. "Just shitty timing."

"Is there ever a good time for a major home repair to come up?" I ask, amusement lacing my words.

"No," he chuckles as he agrees with me. "Thanks again for taking care of everything while I was gone. I can't even imagine what kind of mess it would be if you didn't step in."

"Glad I was here to help."

"Can I take you out to dinner as a way to thank

you?" he asks. I think I detect a sliver of shyness coming out of him with his question.

"I suppose," I say and smile up at him.

"Great. Maybe tomorrow night? I'm pretty jet-lagged today."

"Works for me," I tell him.

"It's a date, then." He smiles at me. I mull his words over as the butterflies in my stomach take flight. I watch as he walks the few feet down the hall and to his door, disappearing inside once he's opened it.

I walk back into my place, closing the door before leaning against it. I still can't believe he referred to tomorrow night as a date. Did he mean it like a real date-date, or just a thank you meal kind of date? I'm so confused. Do I treat this as just a friendly neighborly thank you meal for doing him a favor while gone, or as a hey, I like you and want to get to know you better, kind of meal?

I plop down on my couch and Max immediately jumps up on it, lying down beside me with his head in my lap. I rub the top of his head as we sit here, all the scenarios playing out in my mind as I mull over the conversation with Ryker.

"I know, boy, I don't know what to think, either. Maybe a walk will do us both good," I ramble to my dog. At the word walk, his head perks up and he's ready to launch himself off the couch in search of his leash.

Max jumps off the couch and goes and sits by the door. I can't help but laugh at his excitement as he watches me stand up from the couch again and head for the hook where I keep his leash. I pop into the kitchen and fill both a water bottle for me and the one I carry for him with a little bowl attachment piece, which flips up into a bowl for him when he's ready to drink.

"Let's go," I tell him as I clip the leash to his collar. He knows the drill, walking nicely beside me as we head out, stopping to lock the door behind us, and then we're off on our afternoon adventure.

CHAPTER 9

Ryker

SEPTEMBER

I WRAP the tape around my socks one last time. This is the first time I'm hitting the ice for the first official practice of the Shockwaves. There's been a lot of media coverage leading up to today, and I'm sure it will continue all through camp and into the season. As a veteran player, I'm used to some of the hype, but this feels a little different. With all the excitement and buzz a new team brings to the league, it also brings its own unique level of anticipation and stress to the players. Most new teams struggle for the first few seasons as they work the kinks out.

Normal teams lose and gain just a few of their guys each season, which is easier as a whole to learn chemistry between players. But with the Shock-waves, we've got an entire locker room full of guys who haven't played together, or if they have, it's only a couple, rather than the majority.

"Hey, man," Jason Soaps, one of our rookies, greets as he takes a seat next to me. While I was the first player the Shockwaves picked with the expansion draft, Jason was their first draft pick in the actual draft this past summer.

"How's it going?" I ask him.

"Pretty good. I can't believe we finally made it to today. Seems a little surreal, still," he tells me. I remember back to my first time in an NHL locker room. It was intimidating as shit, but as time went by, it became more and more natural to be in one.

"Have you gotten settled in here?" I ask.

"I'm still in a hotel. Been looking for a place to rent, but also wanted to make it through camp before I pull the trigger on anything long-term. I need to make the final roster before I do anything drastic."

"You'll make it," I tell him confidently. He's a damn good player, and it doesn't hurt that his dad is a future hall of fame member. I got to know his dad a bit with my short stint in Indianapolis, as he's the goalie coach for them after having played there for many years.

"Thanks for your vote of confidence," he says, holding a fist out for me to hit. I do just that as the chatter in the room ramps up as more of the guys fill in and get ready to hit the ice.

I SUCK down a bottle of water, my lungs burning after the practice Coach just put us through. He didn't hold anything back. Some of that is to help show him who's got the potential to actually make his final roster, and some of that was to help dust the cobwebs off our legs. Most guys train all summer, only taking a few weeks off for vacation and such, but there's nothing like the first practice of the season to truly get your blood pumping.

We stand or, in some cases, kneel on the ice in a semi-circle around Coach as he gives his final words to the team before dismissing us until tomorrow.

"Ryker, can you stop by my office once you're showered and dressed?" he asks before I leave the ice.

"Sure can, Coach," I tell him before I head down the tunnel. I have no idea what he might want to see me about, but I try not to worry about it until I'm in his office.

"Getting called to the principal's office already?" Damien Thompson, one of the other veteran players who was picked up by the Shockwaves in the expansion draft, asks. We were in the same draft class, so have kind of come up in this league together.

"I guess so. He didn't seem to be pissed, so I don't think it can be anything bad," I tell him. Brett Jackson was an assistant coach when I was first drafted. He left for a head coaching position a few years later, so we got to know one another pretty well during that time. Granted, that was nearly a decade ago, but still, I remember him being a fair and easy to get along with coach.

I strip out of my sweaty gear before grabbing my shower bag. I wrap a towel around my waist and head for the shower. This facility is brand new, and pretty state of the art. It definitely has the largest locker room I've ever been in. The individual shower stalls are not your normal gym showers. First off, they're private and spacious. The shower-heads are adjustable, and the pressure is amazing. I've showered in some pretty crappy locker rooms in my time, but this one might go down as the best in the league.

I shut the water off, then reach out and grab the towel hanging from the hook. I dry off, then wrap the towel around my hips and head back to my cubby. I pull out my clean clothes, thankful we can come and go to practice in whatever we want. The league dress code of suits is only a game-day requirement. I'm comfortable, once again, this time in a pair of shorts and a T-shirt.

I head for the coach's office, rapping my knuckles on the doorframe before entering the open door.

"Ryker, take a seat," he says as he motions to one of the chairs facing his desk. "How are you settling in?" Brett asks, and I can tell he is actually interested in my answer.

"Pretty good. I bought a place over the summer. I have my daughter living with me, now, so it's been a slight adjustment. Teenagers, man, they are something else." I chuckle, thinking of Ellie. She is mostly a pretty chill kid, but like anyone, she has her moments.

"I know exactly what you mean. My daughter, Brooklyn, is about to turn sixteen and she's giving her mother and me a run for our money."

"Is she liking California?" I ask.

"So far. She wasn't too excited about moving schools, but she's starting to make some friends and settle in."

"That's good. Ellie has lived here in California, but she's always been with her mom full-time. Michelle was offered a promotion this summer, requiring a move, so we gave Ellie the choice to stay put and move in with me or go to Texas with her mom. The idea of not having to change schools, make new friends, was a big draw for her staying here. My only dilemma is who will stay with her when we're on the road?"

"Ahh, that can be difficult. I can always talk to my

wife and see if she can stay at our house, if you need someone in a pinch."

"Thanks, Coach. I'll keep it in mind. I think, for some of the shorter trips, Ellie will go stay with her best friend. They're together almost every day as it is, so it wouldn't be much different."

"That sounds like a solid plan, as well," he states. I watch as he leans back in his desk chair, steepling his fingers together. "I wanted to talk to you today. I've been conversing with powers that be, and we'd like for you to be the team's first captain."

"Oh," I say, not expecting it at all. "I'm honored," I tell him, and I truly am. Being the captain can be a lot of pressure, as everyone looks up to you. You have to lead by example. Some new teams wait to name a captain until someone has shown they deserve it, while other organizations name one right away.

"You have what it takes to lead this team. We know this season is going to be a stumbling block, of sorts, as everyone learns to work together as a team, but you were meant for this position and have the full backing of the coaching and front office staff. I personally talked with Nathan Bailey, the team's owner, and he fully supports this decision, as well."

"I don't know what to say, other than thank you. I'll do all of you proud," I tell him. I take his offered hand, shaking it as the matter is settled.

"We'll make the announcement to the team

tomorrow at practice, and a press conference will take place after, to make it official with the media. The jersey department will be busy tonight and tomorrow night adding the C patches to all your jerseys, those for you to wear, as well as ones for the team store."

"Sounds good," I say as we both stand. Brett follows me out of his office. He heads in the direction of the front offices while I head to the players' parking lot. I still can't quite believe I'll be the leader of this team, but I'm pumped. It was my goal to make it to a California team, one that I could possibly call home until I'm ready to retire. Accepting the captain position means this team has faith in me to be with them for the foreseeable future.

CHAPTER 10

Avery

I SIT on a bench in the dog park, soaking in the September sunshine. The heat has started to subside as the fall weather arrives. I definitely don't mind the slightly cooler days headed our way. I let the deep timber of my current audiobook sweep me away to New York, where the book is set. What I wouldn't give to have a hot guy sweep me off my feet. The best I get these days is Max tripping me up as we walk down the sidewalk.

My book pauses as a text message arrives, my British Siri voice breaking in to alert me to the message.

Text message from Ellie Jorgensen: Hi Avery, I was wondering if you are busy tonight? My dad has a game and I have an extra ticket. My friend was supposed to go, but she's sick and can't go.

I slip my phone out of my pocket and pull up the text message so I can reply.

> Hey Ellie! Sorry to hear about your friend, I hope she feels better soon! I'd love to go with you! When do we need to leave by? I'm out at the park with Max right now, so need time to get him home first.

> My dad has to leave in about 20 minutes, but if you don't mind driving us, we can leave much later and closer to the start of the game. He has to be there hours early.

> That makes complete sense, I can totally drive us.

> Perfect! He said once he gets to the rink he can text or email me a parking pass, so we don't have to worry about where to park.

> Sounds like a plan! Do you want to get dinner first?

> Sure! Or I can just grab something at the rink, whatever works best for you.

> I'll need some dinner, so let's figure it out once I'm back, sound good?

Yep! See you soon!

I put my phone back in my pocket and call Max. He happily comes back to me, letting me clip his leash back onto his collar. I give him a quick drink and then we're off on our way back home.

Once back, I get Max a fresh bowl of water and a small treat bone. He takes the treat and heads for his bed in the living room. I head for my bathroom, taking a quick shower to wash away the sweat and grime from the day.

I pull on a pair of jeans, then settle on a T-shirt and a jean jacket. I don't want to freeze, so I also grab a sweatshirt to take, just in case.

I put out Max's dinner and top off his water before I head out. I lock up and walk next door and knock.

"Hey, Avery," Ellie greets me. She's dressed similar to me, except her shirt is a Shockwaves shirt.

"Thanks for inviting me tonight," I tell her as she leans in and gives me a quick hug.

"I didn't want to go by myself, and with my BFF being sick, I didn't have many people to ask."

"If you ever need someone, I'll happily go. You might have to explain what's happening, since I don't know much about hockey, but I haven't found a sport I don't enjoy watching in person."

"I'll keep that in mind! Dad got me a pass for the entire season."

"Cool. What are you thinking for dinner?" I ask.

"I'm pretty easy, so do we want to go down and park and then just find a place close by?" she suggests.

"That's a perfect idea. I think there are a few burger places around the rink."

We head out, following the GPS to the parking lot for the pass Ryker sent us to use. It has a RESERVED sign plastered across the gate, but thankfully, the bar code on our pass opens the gate, allowing us to enter.

"I think this is the player and family lot," Ellie tells me as we pick a spot.

"With the sign out front, it wouldn't surprise me," I tell her. "Plus, most of these cars look expensive. Ones I'd expect professional athletes to drive."

"I agree. Now, where should we go for dinner?" Ellie asks as we both get out of the car. We exit the parking lot and head down the street until we're in front of the arena. The street is busy with fans as they file in and out of the neighboring bars and restaurants, waiting on the doors to the arena to open.

"Let's try that place," I suggest, pointing to a burger and wings place. We make our way through the busy crowd and, thankfully, snag a table out on the patio. It's the type of place where you order from the counter, and they call out when your order is ready. "What would you like? I'll go order for us."

Ellie checks over the menu, and I think it's cute how she hems and haws over what to pick. "I'll go with the grilled chicken sandwich with no tomato and the curly fries," she tells me.

"And to drink?" I ask.

"Just water, for now. I'll grab a soda once we're in the arena."

"Sounds good. I'll be back in just a few." I head for the counter, thankfully not having to wait in line for more than five or so minutes. I put in our order and wait for it to be called.

"That was fast," Ellie says as I set the tray down on the table.

"It was, and it smells so good, I can't wait to dig in." I take my seat and grab my food and drink from the tray. We both go to town, focusing on eating and not talking until our food is completely gone.

"So, how's school and everything going?" I ask as we make our way over to the rink.

"Good. Classes are getting hard, but that's to be expected as a Junior."

"I remember those days. Do you want to go to college once you graduate, or do you have a plan?"

"Oh yes, I undoubtedly want to go into social work. I plan to get my master's, maybe even my doctorate, one day."

"Wow, that's great you have such ambition and drive. Have you started applying to colleges?"

"I haven't sent in any applications just yet, but I've been looking up a few schools. If I stay in the state, then

I have the chance of getting some scholarships because I'm in the top of my class. I know my dad would pay for my schooling, but I want to cover as much of it as I can, and since I get good grades, it shouldn't be hard to do."

"I completely understand. I got scholarships and grants to help pay for most of my degree. My parents aren't in the same financial situation your dad is, so they couldn't help with much, but I was grateful for what they were able to cover. I graduated with very little school debt. So little, in fact, I've already paid it all off."

"That's impressive. I hear of so many kids graduating with thousands, sometimes even hundreds of thousands of student loan debt, and they can never get out from underneath it."

"You're so right and smart to not want to put yourself in that position."

Once we make it inside, we're ushered to our seats. I'm super impressed, as they are located down by the glass, but in what the usher called a floor-level suite. The suite has thirty-two seats, and we have access to our own private bathroom along with free food and drinks. It's pretty swanky, but doesn't surprise me Ryker would want his daughter somewhere safe if she's going to be attending these games with a friend or by herself.

"Dang, these are sweet," Ellie calls out once we take our seats.

"Hi, you must be Ellie," a lady stops next to us, and speaks to Ellie.

"Hi, yes, that's me," she says kindly.

"I'm Holly Jackson, Coach Jackson's wife. He mentioned you one night, said your dad and him had a little conversation and you came up. We have a daughter, Brooklyn, who's just a little bit older than you, I believe. He mentioned you might need someone to stay with every once in a while, and I just wanted to come to introduce myself and let you know you're always welcome at our house."

"Thank you, and that's good to know," Ellie tells her. I didn't even think about the fact Ryker will be traveling all the time and that means Ellie will need someone to stay with. "Is your daughter here tonight?"

"No, she's not much of a hockey fan," Holly laughs. "She's actually out with her girlfriends, tonight. They're having a sleepover for someone's birthday."

"Oh, fun. Maybe we can meet sometime," Ellie tells her.

"I'm sure she'd love that. I'll figure out a good time and let you know. If you want, we can exchange numbers and text to figure everything out," Holly suggests.

"That'd be great," Ellie says, and pulls her phone out. They exchange numbers before Holly goes to her own seat. As more and more people fill in, I realize this suite is for the players' family members, which makes me feel a little out of place. I know I'm here because of Ellie, but it still is a little strange. Everyone is super nice and doesn't even bat an eye when they find out my connection to the team.

"SHOCKWAVES! SHOCKWAVES! SHOCKWAVES!" the crowd chants as the final seconds tick down. The team played like they'd been together for years, completely surprising the away team with a shutout to open their inaugural season and home opener. The final score was three to zero, three different guys scored, Ryker, being the first.

"That was so awesome!" Ellie yells as the final buzzer sounds. "My dad's going to be so pumped!"

"I bet he will be," I tell her as I stand and cheer along with the twenty thousand other fans in the arena. The announcer calls out the three stars of the game as the crowd goes wild as each name is called.

We watch as the guys come out onto the ice and toss a few pucks over the glass to waiting fans, Ryker, being one of them. He gives Ellie a little wave as he passes by our section, and she calls out to him, "Love you, Dad!"

I watch as he skates back to the bench, where he sits down on it as he's handed a microphone. His face flashes up on the jumbotrons as the rink-side reporter starts to ask him some questions.

"Ryker, great game out there tonight. How did it feel to score the first-ever Shockwaves goal?"

"That was pretty surreal, something I don't think I'll ever forget."

"How does it feel to wear the team's C and lead this group of guys?"

"It is an incredible honor the ownership and management trusted me with. One I take seriously. I'll fight for this team and that locker room full of guys every time I step out on this ice. Being the new team in the league isn't going to be easy, but we're here to make it happen and hope at the end of our first season, we've got more wins than losses and we can stand up as the inaugural team and be proud to be a member of this team."

"Thanks for your time tonight, and congratulations on the first win of the season," the reporter tells him. He hands the microphone back and takes off down the tunnel.

"Did you want to head home or stick around until your dad is ready?" I ask Ellie.

"I'm good either way. If you need to get home to let Max out, we can go."

"He should be fine for a little bit longer. Do you know how long he usually is?"

"It can sometimes be a while, especially if he has to do any press conferences."

"Oh, then yeah, we can head back."

We say our goodbyes to the other people in our suite before we make our way out to the parking lot. Since we're in a different location than all the fan parking, we easily slip out and are back on the highway toward home pretty quickly.

"Would you like to come out with me while I walk Max?" I ask Ellie as I pull into the parking garage.

"Sure, I'll just text my dad and let him know where I'm at," she says as she pulls her phone out and taps on the screen.

We head upstairs, and as soon as my key turns the lock, I can hear Max on the other side of the door. He's usually right there waiting to greet me when I return home, and today is no different.

"Max, were you a good boy?" I ask him as he sits so I can attach his leash. His tail is wagging back and forth so fast, so I know he's excited, especially since Ellie is with me.

"Hey, Max," she greets him, scratching the top of his head. "He's so loveable," she comments.

"He sure is. I'm so glad I made the decision to get him when I did. He's brought so much joy to my life."

"I bet. I wonder if I could convince my dad to get us a dog?" Ellie muses.

"Maybe. They can be a lot of work, but it is so worth it. They truly are man's best friends."

We take Max on a short walk, where he quickly does his business before we return back to the condo building.

"Would you like to come in until your dad gets home, or I can come over to your place to hang out?"

"Are you sure? I've already taken up so much of your time," Ellie says.

"I wouldn't have offered if I didn't mean it. I have nothing better to do, just sit and binge some trash TV."

"What is your favorite to binge?" she asks, her excitement noticeable.

"A little bit of everything! I love-love the Bachelor franchise. I don't think I've ever skipped a season. I also love cooking and baking shows and the singing ones, as well."

"I swear, you're just an older version of me—minus never having missed a season of the bachelor, since it started airing before I was born, but my mom always watched it, so I'd watch it with her sometimes," she says and I can tell she's a little sad now that she brought her mom up.

"I bet you miss her," I state, not truly a question. We head inside my place, letting Max off his leash before making our way to the couch.

"Yeah, it's been kind of weird adjusting to being with my dad all the time and only talking to my mom. I've only ever known it the other way around. Don't get me wrong, I'm enjoying getting more time with him. Our relationship has only strengthened, but I miss my mom. We'd sit up and just talk, or go shopping or to dinner and the movies."

"Do you know when you'll get to see her next?" I ask.

"Next month! We have fall break and I'm flying out for the few days I'm off. She made sure she'd be home for those days, even took a couple of days off so we can spend as much time together as possible."

"That will be so much fun," I tell her.

"It will, and it works out perfectly since my dad is on a road trip that week."

"Sounds like it was kismet."

"Do you see your family often?" she asks.

"I do. My parents live about ninety minutes away. I usually see them once every four to six weeks. I have one brother, but he lives in Colorado, so I don't see him as much."

"Nice. I sometimes wish I'd had a sibling."

"I wished I was an only child many days," I say, laughing at our complete opposite situations. "Until later, and then my brother and I became better friends. But during our childhood, we fought like only brothers and sisters can fight."

"Who's older?" she asks.

"He is, by sixteen months," I tell her.

"Ah, and let me guess, he tried to play the big brother card all the time?"

"Pretty much, and was always pestering me when

my friends were over. It was so annoying," I huff out, thinking back to those days.

"My best friend Stephanie's brother, Jordan, is like that. The only difference is he's three years younger than she is. He always wants to bother us when we're hanging out."

"Maybe he has a crush on you, that happens often."

"Yuck, I sure hope not." She scrunches up her face in disgust and I can't help but laugh.

"I should have asked when we got back, but do you need anything? A drink or snack?" I offer.

"I'm good, but thanks. I do, however, need to use your restroom, if it's okay?" she asks.

"Of course, it's just down the hall, first door on the right."

"Thanks, I'll be right back."

I check my phone and it's already almost eleven o'clock at night. No wonder why I'm tired. Just as Ellie returns to the living room, a knock sounds at the door, which has Max up and barking at the noise.

"Settle, Max," I call out to him, and he does as he's told. He might not like it, but he sits at attention on his mat in the living room. I check the peephole before opening the door and find Ryker on the other side, a suit that fits him to perfection on his body, with an un-tied tie around his neck.

"Hey," he casually greets as he steps inside. I close the door behind him and turn to find him crouched down on his haunches petting a very happy Max, who apparently decided I didn't mind if he left his mat to come say hi to Ryker.

"Great game tonight. Thanks for the tickets and parking pass."

"Thanks for bringing Ellie. I'm glad it worked out for you to join her last minute," he says, standing back up to his full height.

"I told her any time she needed someone to join her, I'm available."

"Good to know," he muses.

"Dad, we've got a slight problem for Sunday," Ellie tells him as she pockets her cell.

"What's that?" he asks.

"Not only is Steph sick, but now her brother and mom have both started to show signs of having the flu, as well. They don't think it's a good idea if I go stay there for the two nights you'll be gone."

"Shit, okay, we'll figure it out in the morning," he says, scrubbing his face. She didn't tell me any of this, so I'm caught just as off guard as Ryker is.

"I can stay with you," I offer, and they both turn to look at me.

"Really?!" Ellie asks, and I think I hear a hint of excitement.

"Absolutely. I'm here and I don't mind making sure you get fed and off to school and back home again."

"You'd be doing me a huge favor if you're truly okay with it," Ryker says.

"I'm one thousand-percent sure. If you give me a list of all your away trips, I can probably cover all of them for you. It isn't like you live far from me. If you're comfortable with it, Ellie can still sleep in her own bed, I can sleep in mine, and we check in with each other, as needed. If you'd prefer we sleep in the same condo, we can figure out whose place is best and go from there."

"That is a huge time commitment for you to take on," Ryker brings up.

"Ryker, as I told Ellie earlier, I only offer to help when I know I can help. Ellie being able to sleep in her own bed on school nights is a giant plus when you're on the road. Just say 'thank you, Avery,' and send me a copy of your schedule and we can go from there."

"You're a godsend," he tells me, and I can't stop the blush creeping up my neck at his words.

"How about we give it a try for this trip and, if everything goes well, we can plan for the rest," I suggest.

"I'm fine with it," Ellie pipes up.

Ryker looks between his daughter and me before speaking, "Let's give it a test run and reassess next week. It will also give me time to talk things over with Michelle and make sure she's okay with this arrangement," he states. "It will also give you a chance to figure out what compensation you'd like for your time," he says directly to me.

"Oh, I wasn't expecting to be paid," I tell him honestly. "Maybe just make sure Ellie has food in the house and we can figure everything out."

"I can't expect you to watch my daughter and not be compensated for your time," he insists.

"Okay, I'll think of something," I tell him, just to get him off the topic.

"Thanks again for coming with me tonight. I had a great time," Ellie tells me as she stops to give me a hug before following her dad out the door.

"Anytime. I had fun," I tell her as they walk the short distance to their own door. Once they've gone inside, I close and lock up. I take Max out on the balcony and let him use the small grass box I had installed for easy potty breaks when I can't get him out on a walk, or for our last chance to pee for the night.

With him securely tucked into his kennel, I make my way into my bedroom to get myself ready. The exhaustion hits me hard as I use the bathroom. I crawl into bed a few minutes later, too tired to even read a few pages of my book.

CHAPTER 11

Ryker

I HEAD INTO MY ROOM, stripping my suit off as I go. I still can't believe we won tonight, and I scored the first goal of the season. I told the guys before we hit the ice to just play the game like they know how to play. Win or lose, I'd be proud of them, and proud I was. Everyone was on fire tonight. I think they felt like we had something to prove.

I slip into some shorts and a T-shirt before heading back out to the living room. "Did you have a good time tonight?" I ask Ellie. She's curled up on the couch, a blanket covering her as she watches some cooking show on TV.

"So fun. I genuinely like Avery. She's so nice."

"I'm glad you've made a friend."

"We went to dinner before going to the arena. I didn't realize we'd have food provided to us in the suite," she tells me.

"Now you know for future games. What do you think of her offer to watch over you while I'm gone?" I ask.

"I actually like the idea. It keeps me home, and my schedule as normal as possible. That's not to say I won't want to go to Steph's some weekends, but I can definitely see the perks of it for trips during the week that are school nights."

"I'd hate to take advantage of her generosity."

"I don't think she'd offer if she wasn't okay with it."

"That's what she says now, but the season is long, and I play half of it on the road."

"Let's just take it road trip by road trip and see how things go."

"Sometimes your maturity blows me out of the water. Where did my little girl with pigtails go?"

"I grew up, Dad," she says, all while rolling her eyes at me.

"There's my sassy teenager." I chuckle.

"Whatever." She rolls her eyes again, but can't hold back the laugh that also follows it.

"Unless you need something, I'm off to bed. I'm exhausted and need a good night's sleep. We can hit up the store tomorrow for some food before I leave town, and get things set in place."

"Sounds like a plan. I'm not far behind you tonight. I'm getting pretty sleepy myself," she tells me before standing up to come give me a hug goodnight. I press a kiss to the top of her head before I let her go. I don't think she'll get to my height, seeing as how she hardly reaches my shoulders. Curse of having a short mom, I guess.

"Night, Ellie Bean. I love you," I call out as I walk down the hall.

"Love you, too, Dad," she replies.

I showered at the rink, so there's no need to do it again at home. After brushing my teeth and using the bathroom quick, I strip down to my boxer briefs and slide between the cold sheets. They feel good on my hot skin. My muscles are still screaming at me that I haven't used them to play a full game in months now. We have pre-season games, but as the captain and a for-sure final roster player, I didn't play much of the games. They are the final parts of camp where the coaching staff gets their eyes on the guys who are fighting for the final roster spots and being sent down to the minors. Not everyone invited to camp can make the final list. I remember those days, and thankfully, they're far behind me at this point in my career.

Sleep claims me fairly quickly, as it usually does after a hard-fought game like we had tonight.

"Morning, Dad," Ellie greets me as I make my way into the kitchen. She's got a few mixing bowls out and the counter covered in some kind of dough. I stumble my way over to the coffee pot, dropping a pod in and place a cup underneath before turning it on.

"Morning, Ellie Bean. What are you making?" I ask as the coffee starts gurgling to life.

"Cinnamon rolls," she says, looking over her shoulder at me quickly. "And once they go in the oven, I'll start some sausage."

"You're certainly taking to this cooking thing," I tell her. Ever since we returned from our vacation this summer, she's taken to cooking most of our meals.

"I enjoy it, and they made these on the show I was watching last night. I'd never tried making them from scratch, but they made it look so easy. It hasn't been hard, yet, so I'm hoping it stays that way," she tells me as I watch her start to roll the cinnamon-sugar and butter-covered dough up in a long roll. Once she has it all rolled together, she scores the dough in the increments she wants it sliced in, then goes back through and cuts the rolls into the desired thickness. I watch as she transfers the rolls onto a greased baking dish, filling it with all the rolls she cut.

My coffee finishes brewing, so I add a little bit of creamer before taking the first hot sip. I can practically feel the caffeine hit my bloodstream as it starts to wake me up. "What are we going to do with all of these cinnamon rolls?" I question as she fills a second pan up.

"I figured I'd take some over to Avery. The others we can try freezing to eat another time."

"All good plans," I state.

"Have you started a list of things we need at the store today?" I ask.

"Not yet, but once I have the kitchen cleaned up and the sausage made, I can."

"I don't know what I did to get such a great daughter, but I wouldn't trade you for anything in the world," I tell her as I give her a quick side hug and kiss to her temple.

"Even a son who could follow in your footsteps and play hockey?" she asks, and I'm kind of shocked.

"Not even close. You were—scratch that—are the best thing that has happened to me. Better than being drafted, better than playing ten-plus seasons in the NHL, better than making the Olympic team a few years ago and medaling at the games. I'd give it all up if you needed me to."

"I'd never need you to."

"I know, but I also know I've missed a shit-ton of your childhood due to my career. I hope you know how much it killed me over the years to be so far away from you all the time. I did it for you, just as much as I was doing it for myself. It was my dream from the time I could hardly skate to make it to the NHL, then once I did, I pushed myself to stay there so I could provide the best life you could possibly live."

"Mom did her best to make it so I wouldn't realize I could have whatever I wanted. She wanted me to believe I was like every other middle-class family who lived around us."

"There's nothing wrong with that mentality. I've seen some teammates whose kids were spoiled brats, who would throw a fit if they didn't have the *'it'* product or outfit the moment it was available. I couldn't ever see you acting that way, and I'm thankful you don't."

"I'm thankful Mom and you raised me that way. I've never felt like I didn't have what I needed, and that's more than some people can say."

"Are you sure you're only fifteen?" I tease. Ellie has always been mature beyond her years, always worried about those less fortunate. I can remember many times she'd want to stop and give every person we passed on the road holding a sign stating they needed money for food or something their sign requested. We'd do it sometimes, or go and make up some kits with snacks, maybe some clean socks, and a gift card or two for local fast-food places.

"I had an idea," she says, turning to face me with a mischievous look on her face.

"Why do I feel like I'm not going to like this idea?" I ask, squaring myself up to my daughter.

"Just hear me out," she instructs. "I think you should ask Avery out on a date."

"Why's that?" I ask, not knowing where this is coming from.

"Because she's nice, and she's pretty, and I'm ninety-nine percent positive you like her more than just as a friendly neighbor."

"What makes you believe that?" I ask.

"I've noticed how you look at her, and your voice does this little shift when you talk to her. You're sweet on her, even if you don't realize it."

"I am?" I question.

"Yes!" she practically cries out. "I think you'd look cute together as a couple."

"And if it doesn't work out, wouldn't it be weird to live next door to each other?"

"But what if it does. Just think of the meet-cute you'd have."

"I can't believe my daughter is giving me dating advice," I say, staring at the ceiling as I ponder her advice.

"Just think about it. I'm not saying you have to marry her, but a date to see how compatible you are won't hurt."

"We went out to dinner one night after she took care of the leak while we were gone." I toss it out for good measure.

"Yeah, with me and Steph in tow. That wasn't a date, by any means. I want the glitz and glamor of you getting dressed up and taking her to a swanky restaurant that usually requires a six-month reservation, but who will drop everything to give you a table because you're the captain of the new hometown team. Then, out for a romantic walk on the boardwalk. You can end it with a goodnight kiss at her door…or I can arrange to spend the night at Steph's, so you have the place to yourself for any other activities you might want the house empty for."

Did my daughter just insinuate I need to get laid? My mind must be playing tricks on me because there's no way she just insinuated it.

"That was a lot to take in and digest. All I'll say is, I'll think about it," I tell her before slinking out of the kitchen. I don't need to be having discussions about my sex life with my daughter.

"Here's everything you might possibly need while I'm gone. There's a letter giving you permission to seek medical treatment should something come up, along with copies of our medical cards. I've also included the phone numbers of her doctor, dentist, pharmacy, the hotel I'll be at, a few of the coaching staff and support staff's cell numbers, should you need something and I don't answer my cell. I've also left one of my credit cards in there if you need to buy anything. Just use the card or, if they won't let you, just let me know the total and I'll reimburse you ASAP," I rattle off to Avery like I'm a madman.

"We'll be fine, Ryker. Go and have a good trip away. If anything goes wrong, I can handle it."

"I know, sorry. I trust you. I absolutely do. But I've just never had to deal with this."

"Take a deep breath, go say goodbye to your daughter, and leave," Avery insists, pulling out what I can only equate to a mom's voice, even though she isn't a mom.

"Yes, ma'am. I'll see you in a couple of days. Thanks again."

"You're welcome. Kick some ass while you're gone," she calls out to my retreating back.

"How did that go?" Ellie asks as I walk back in.

"She wasn't amused." I cringe.

"I told you." She laughs.

"Yeah, yeah," I state. "All right, I've got to get going. You be good, call me when you can or if you need anything."

"I'll be fine, Dad," she reminds me.

"Love you, Ellie Bean," I tell her as I pull her into a bear hug. She squeezes me back, and I know deep down she'll be just fine. "See you in a few days, behave yourself."

"Always," she states.

I grab the handle of my suitcase and wheel it out the door. She follows me out and I watch as she heads to Avery's door. She knocks twice before walking in. I hustle to the elevator as I can't be late for our first road trip, wouldn't be very responsible of me.

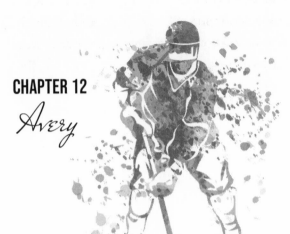

CHAPTER 12

Avery

"I DIDN'T THINK he'd ever leave," Ellie says as she sits down on my couch. Max doesn't wait for permission as he jumps up on the couch and lies across her lap. She happily pats his head and body, giving him the love and attention he was after.

"It was kind of cute how nervous he was when he brought me the envelope." I giggle and tell her about it.

"Oh god, how embarrassing," she says, covering part of her face with her one free hand.

"Not embarrassing. It just goes to show the level of love he has for you."

"I guess. I hope he isn't like that for every trip."

"My guess is once the first one goes well, he'll mellow out."

"And if he doesn't?" she questions.

"We give him a swift kick to the ass and tell him to pull up his big-boy boxers and figure his shit out."

"God, I love your straight-shooting personality."

"I've learned how to assert myself over the years. It's one of my strengths."

"I can see that," she tells me. "I told my dad he should ask you out on a date," she says as I start to take a drink of water, but it comes out, spraying all over me.

"You what?" I question, making sure I heard her okay.

"I told him he should take you out on a date. You know, dinner, romantic walk on the beach, maybe a movie or play, followed by a goodnight kiss at your door or maybe inside…" She trails off.

"And what did he say to that?" I ask, curious what his reaction to her suggestion might be.

"He said he'd think about it," she tells me, and I can feel my confidence falter just a little bit. "I think my insinuating I could make sure I wasn't around in case you guys wanted to come back home and spend the night together made him a little uncomfortable," she tells me, twisting her hands like she's nervous telling me that.

"I could see how it would be uncomfortable." I smirk. "Maybe no more comments about that?" I suggest.

"I think you're right," she agrees.

"What did you want to do today?" I ask,

changing the subject. As much as I want to fantasize about a night in Ryker's bed, I can't do so with his daughter in front of me.

"Dad and I went grocery shopping yesterday, so we have plenty of food for the next few days. What if we headed to the mall? I'd actually like to get a pedicure, maybe one of the places there can take me as a walk-in."

"Sure, we can head there. I need to take Max out quick, and then we can go. Do you want to come with me?" I offer.

"I'll stay here. I need to run next door and grab my things. I can meet you back in twenty, does that work?"

"Sure," I agree and clip-on Max's leash.

THE HOT WATER heats my skin, relaxing my muscles as I sit here. We found a nail place after arriving at the mall. Thankfully, they were able to fit both of us in as walk-ins for a pedicure this afternoon. Ellie is in the chair to my right, also enjoying the relaxation the hot water brings.

"Best idea ever," she tells me as the massage part of her chair kicks in.

"I'd have to agree. I needed a pedicure so bad. I haven't been in forever."

"Look this way and smile," she instructs, and I do as she said. She snaps a picture of the two of us, tapping away on her screen. A second later, my own phone chimes and I see she's started a group text between her dad, and the two of us.

ELLIE

We're out having a girls' day at the mall. Thanks for the credit card, dad. {winky smile face}

I chuckle at her caption. "You know I can pay for myself," I tell her as I heart the picture and save it to my phone.

"I know, but my dad gave me his card and said to pay for anything I can when we're together."

"I'll let it slide this time, but in the future, I'd prefer paying for myself."

"Okay, I can work with that."

We exchange a few words as we're both worked on. The massage I get practically puts me to sleep in the chair.

An hour and a half later, we're both ready to go. I don't argue when Ellie hands over Ryker's credit card to pay for our pedicures. "Want to grab a snack? I'm craving one of those pretzels we smelled baking this entire time."

"Sure, I'm also hungry, thanks to the smell." She chuckles as we make our way over to the pretzel stand. We each get one, along with cups of cheese to dip them into.

"Want to sit down or keep walking?" I ask once we both have our items.

"Let's sit, that way, we don't accidentally spill on something."

I find a table and wipe the surface off with one of the napkins in my hand before we sit down. "So, what's your schedule like tomorrow? Do I need to be up by a certain time to make sure you get out of bed?"

"I should be fine, I've got my two alarms, plus, I'm a morning person."

"Okay, what time do you get up?"

"My first alarm goes off at six."

"Dang, what time do you start school?" I question.

She laughs and takes another bite from her pretzel. "First period starts at seven fifty-five. I usually like to get there around seven forty. It gives me time to ready myself for my first class. If I'm rushed in the morning, it just throws off my entire day."

"I'm the same way. I like things consistent, that way I know what to expect and when to expect it. What time are you done with school?" I ask.

"School ends at two thirty-five, but I have my drama club after school tomorrow, so I won't be home until close to four."

"Do you need a ride?"

"No, I just walk home. My school is only a few blocks away."

"If that changes, just give me a call," I offer.

"Thanks, but I'll be fine. I walk most of the way with some friends who live nearby."

"Is drama the only after-school club you're in?"

"Yep. Last year I also went to the Spanish club, but since I'm not taking the class this year, I gave it up."

"Do you play any sports?"

"No, but I do manage the volleyball team."

"Fun! What does that require you to do?" I ask.

"I help keep track of player stats, make sure things are all set up for practice, help the players with any uniform issues they might have, things like that. It makes me feel part of the team, but I don't actually play. I'd much rather be on the sidelines than out on the court," she tells me.

"I'm the same way, not very athletic."

We finish up our snack and walk around the mall for a little while, checking out a few stores as we go.

"Did you find everything you wanted?" I ask Ellie as we near the doors.

"I think so, and if not, I'll get it the next time I come."

"Sounds good. Shall we head back home? We can figure out what we want for dinner and then call it an early evening."

"That works for me," she agrees.

"Hello," I greet as I bring my cell to my ear.

"Hi. How were things today?" Ryker asks.

"Horrible. Ellie wouldn't listen, she ran away, then came back and trashed my place. I just don't know what to do." I try and pull off my lie, but the laughter breaks out, many thanks to Ellie's laughter right next to me.

"Ha-ha, very funny," Ryker deadpans.

"Today was great. We went to the mall, got pedicures, which you already know about since Ellie texted you. After that, we shopped our way through the mall and then came home. We just finished some chicken fettuccine alfredo and are settling in to watch the newest episode of *The Voice*."

"Sounds like a good day. How much of my money did my daughter spend?" he asks, but I can tell he doesn't actually care.

"Not much. I think she only bought a few things from two stores. Maybe a hundred bucks or so, not counting the trip to the nail salon. Thanks, by the way. She insisted you wanted to pay."

"You're welcome. And I did insist. Figured you couldn't say no to my kid." He snickers.

"Sneaky sneaky, Mr. Jorgensen."

"It's the least I could do. You're helping me out more than you know."

"Well, as I told Ellie, I'd let it slide this time, but I can pay for myself. I don't need your money, Ryker."

"And I appreciate that. Not many people would pass up access to someone else's credit card with no limit on how much they can spend with it."

"I'll let you in on a little secret, money doesn't impress me."

"Good to know," he says. "Are you ladies all set for tomorrow?"

"We are. We already discussed Ellie's schedule and what time she needs to leave and what time I should expect her home since she's got stuff after school."

"Sounds like you've got everything under control."

"Now you're catching on," I tease him.

"Avery's doing just fine, Dad," Ellie calls out, and I quickly switch my phone to speaker so he can hear her.

"I know, but it doesn't change the fact I'm still your dad and worried something is going to happen, and I won't be there."

"And if something does go wrong, Avery is a big girl, Dad. She can take care of it."

"Thanks for your vote of confidence," I tell her as we high-five.

"Why do I feel like I'm being ganged up on?" Ryker asks.

"Because you're being over the top," Ellie tells him.

"I love you, too, Ellie Bean," he deadpans.

"Love you, Dad," she sing-songs back to him. I love seeing this side of their relationship.

"All right, I get it. Everything is good and you're both doing just fine without me there."

"You finally get it," Ellie quips and I can't help but laugh again at her sassy comebacks.

"Hey now, take it easy on your old man," Ryker tells her, and we both look at each other and just roll our eyes.

"Dad, how many times do I have to tell you? You aren't old. Right, Avery?" She locks eyes with me, a pleading look willing me to agree with her.

"Right. You are way off from being old. I don't even consider my dad old, and he's got a few decades on you."

"You both are good for my ego," he says, and I can practically hear the smirk in his voice.

"We do our best," I tell him.

"All right, I'll let the two of you get back to your show. Have a good day at school tomorrow, Ellie. And have a good workday, Avery."

"We will, and I'll text you when I'm out of school," Ellie tells him.

"Sounds good. I'll probably already be on the ice, or at least away from my phone, but I'll get it when I can. Are you ladies planning on watching the game?"

"I'll have to check if I can even get it," I tell him.

"If you don't have it, you can go over to my place and watch it. I've got the package that shows all games no matter where you are."

"Good to know," I tell him.

"All right, good night, ladies. Love you, Ellie," Ryker says.

"Love you, too, Dad. Good night," she tells him.

"Night. Have a good game tomorrow!" I add before the line goes dead.

"Well, it went better than I expected it to. I think he's finally calmed down and realized we weren't going to burn the place down on the first day."

"I agree," I reply. "Shall we get to watching the show?"

"Yep," Ellie agrees, and we both turn our attention to the TV. We discuss each contestant as they shoot their shot up on the stage, hoping for at least one chair to turn for them.

"All right, I'm going to head home and get to bed. I'll let you know I'm leaving in the morning," Ellie says as she stands from the couch and stretches.

"Sounds good, and if you need me before then, call, text, come over, whatever works. I'll make sure to have my ringer and text notifications on during the night, so I hear them if you need me."

"Thanks," she says, and leans in for a hug. "I genuinely hope you and my dad end up together. I think you'd be good for him, and I wouldn't have to worry about him dating some puck bunny who'd treat me like crap."

"Aw, sweetie. I'd hope no one would do that to you. But you never know, stranger things have happened," I tell her. I think it is sweet how much she's trying to set her dad up, and I don't mind one bit she thinks so highly of me that she's pushing him my way.

CHAPTER 13

Ryker

I collect the puck from behind our net and look down the ice to see what my guys are doing. Aiden Fox, my center, and Jason Soaps, my other winger, is in the neutral zone, both fighting to get open for a cross-ice pass. Tristan Henderson and Damien Thompson, our defensive line currently on the ice, also work at breaking up the neutral zone as I bring the puck closer.

I see my sliver of an opening, punching the puck through one of Edmonton's forwards' feet. I skate around him, collecting the puck just before we drop into our offensive zone.

Edmonton's players drop back, doing their best to close off the center lanes. I pass the puck to Damien, who quickly passes it to Tristan. He sends a one-timer toward the net, only for the Edmonton goalie to reach his hand out and snap the puck out of the air.

"Fuck!" I yell as we just can't seem to get one past him tonight. We're deep in the third period and trailing by one. If we don't score sometime in the next three minutes, we'll face our first loss of the season and our first shutout. Not a great way to start a two-game road trip.

I skate back to the bench, allowing a fresh set of guys to hit the ice. They fight hard but don't get the puck into the back of the net.

The locker room is on the quiet side as we all file in, defeat sets in. We've all been here before, but this one feels different, for some reason. Maybe because it's the franchise's first regular-season loss, or because we fought so hard out there for sixty minutes and couldn't score once. Thankfully, our goalie, Blake Watson, was playing like a beast and only let the one goal in.

"Can I have everyone's attention, please," Coach Jackson calls as he enters the locker room. "You all played great out there tonight. This one just didn't go our way. We didn't give up, and that shows how everyone is taking this loss. This might have been our first one of the season, but it surely won't be the last. Keep your chin up and let this one just roll off your back. Tomorrow is a new day and I'm proud to call you my team," he says to the room at large.

His pep talk works wonders. As everyone starts stripping from their gear, the noise level goes up.

Guys start joking and having a good time as we all go through our post-game ritual.

Once I'm showered and dressed, I finally get a chance to check my cell. I've got a couple of missed text messages. One from Ellie, letting me know she was home from school, another from her and Avery, a picture attached showing me as they ate some pizza while watching the game. She even timed the picture just right so that I'm in it on the TV screen. I can't help but chuckle at it.

I reply back to the group text, since I know they're together.

RYKER

> Looks like it was a fun night. How was school today, Ellie?

ELLIE

> It was good, sorry about the game. {sad face}

> Thanks, we played hard and that's all I can ask of these guys.

AVERY

> Sorry about the loss, you played hard. You guys got robbed so many times tonight. Nothing was getting past their goalie.

> Tell me about it. He was a brick wall tonight.

I slip my phone back into my pocket, as it's time to get loaded up on the bus that will take us to the airplane. We're flying tonight to Chicago, for our game there.

Once on the bus, I pull my phone back out to see if I've missed any other messages from them. I notice Avery has texted me directly, and not from our group one.

AVERY

Just a heads up, Ellie has dropped the idea a few times she hopes you ask me out and that we start dating. I haven't really responded much to her comments to try and not encourage or lead her on. I just didn't want you to be blindsided by it or think I was putting her up to it.

So, is that a no before I can even ask?

I quickly hit send, not allowing myself time to think my response over. The bubbles immediately pop up as she types her reply. I hate the anticipation while I wait for her words to come up. The bubbles play tricks on me as they disappear, only to pop up again, a few seconds later.

"What are you waiting on?" Aiden asks as he drops into the seat next to me.

"Just a reply from my neighbor. She's watching Ellie for me this trip."

"Ah, and how is that all working out?" he questions.

"From the phone call I had with them last night and the text conversation, they seem to be just fine. It helps they get along so well. I think Ellie likes having someone who isn't a parent, but more like an older sister to hang out with. With this setup, it is also allowing her to be home at night, so her normal routine isn't jacked up."

"That's smart. I don't know how people handle having families or kids with the schedule we keep. It is brutal."

"You're telling me. She was born so early in my professional career that it is all I know."

My phone lighting up pulls my attention back to the screen, and I immediately click on the text notification so I can see her entire reply.

> Are you asking me out on a formal date, Mr. Jorgensen? If so, I accept. I'm free Friday or Saturday night just as a heads up. {winky face}

> Ms. Reid, mark your calendar. I'm going to sweep you off your feet come Friday night. Better yet, mark both days as busy. If I'm anything it is confident, and I have a feeling we'll be ready for date number two on Saturday.

Confident. I like it, it is sexy.

> Is there any way you can talk Ellie into staying over at Steph's this weekend?

I'll see what I can do.

> You're the best.

I switch back to the group text, so I can talk to both of them at the same time.

RYKER

> We're headed for the airport. It will be late when we arrive in Chicago, so I'm just saying goodnight here and now. If you want to call in the morning, Ellie, I should be available when you're up and getting ready for school.

ELLIE

Will do, Dad. Have a safe flight and a good night. Love you.

RYKER

Love you, too, night.

I slip my phone back into my pocket. The drive over to the airport isn't a long one, so there's no sense in starting a movie on my iPad or phone. I can do that once we're in the air and on our way to the next city.

SPLITTING a two-game road trip isn't bad. We rallied against Chicago, scoring our game-winning goal with only ten seconds left. Their goalie was pissed and tried to sell the refs on calling a goaltender inter-ference penalty against Damien. Their coaching staff obviously thought he was onto something as they challenged the goal, but lost the challenge when it was reviewed.

As soon as the game ended tonight and everyone was showered and changed, we headed straight back to the airport and flew home. It was the middle of the night before we touched down, and I'm exhausted as I make my way home.

I quietly unlock the door, bringing my suitcase inside, but leaving it there at the entrance. I can deal with the contents once I've gotten a few hours of sleep in me.

Ellie's door is shut as I walk past, so I don't look in on her. I'd hate to wake her up at this time of the morning. I push into my room, finding it looking just as I left it. The sheet and blanket were a jumbled mess on the mattress. A few dress shirts were tossed on the top of my dresser, and two of the drawers are open a few inches as if I packed in a hurry when I left.

I strip from my suit, adding it to the pile on my dresser. I'll need to collect things and take them to the dry cleaners sometime this week, as my pile is already starting to grow.

I plug my phone in, then place it on the nightstand. Sleep is calling my name, so I slide into bed, fix the sheets and comforter once I'm in my spot, and quickly fall asleep.

"MORNING, DAD," I hear Ellie whisper from my doorway.

"Morning, Ellie Bean," I groggily call out, only able to crack my eyes open a sliver.

"I'm off to school, just wanted to say hi. I'll talk to you later."

"Love you. Have a good day and I should be here when you get home."

"See you then," she says before walking down the

hall. I stay awake long enough to hear her leave, stopping to lock the door after she exits.

When I wake, the sun is high in the sky. It's a good thing we had today off after getting in so late last night. I don't sleep the best when we're on the road. Hotel room beds aren't the highest quality, so after a few days, my body is usually screaming for my mattress.

I stumble to the kitchen and find a little note stuck to the coffee machine from Ellie.

It's all ready for you, just press start! Hope you have a good day. Maybe you should surprise Avery with some lunch, or an afternoon walk in the park.

My kid sure is trying to play matchmaker, it appears. Not that I don't like her idea.

I suck down a cup of coffee, the caffeine hitting my bloodstream and giving me the much-needed jolt of energy I need today. I take a quick shower, then get dressed in a Shockwaves T-shirt and a pair of jeans.

I pull a ball cap down low on my head, hoping to help disguise myself as much as I can. I've been spotted before when I run out for errands. It is part of the job, but sometimes I don't have time to sit and talk to a dozen fans.

I run into a little bistro just a couple of blocks from the condo, ordering two of the daily lunch specials and two smoothies.

With food in hand, I head back, but instead of

heading to my unit, I knock on Avery's door, hoping I've arrived before she's already eaten lunch today.

It only takes her a minute or so after I knock to answer.

"Hey," she greets as she pulls the door open. Avery gives me a little wave as she steps aside, giving me the invitation to enter. Max is sitting patiently on his bed in the corner. His tail is going a mile a minute, giving away just how excited he is to see me.

"Hey. I thought I'd bring some lunch over," I tell her as I set things down on the counter.

"Thanks. I was just thinking about lunch as my stomach started to growl."

"Well, it's a good thing I showed up when I did." I smile down at her before turning to open the bag and unpack our food.

We each grab a to-go container, taking them to her table. "Would you like something to drink besides the smoothie?" she asks.

"A water is fine," I tell her. I watch as she walks back to the kitchen, my eyes never leaving the sway of her walking away.

"How was your trip?" Avery asks as she sets two glasses filled with ice water down in front of our boxes.

"Pretty good. Not much different than the hundreds of other trips I've taken during my career."

"What's it like being on the road? Do you get much downtime?" she asks.

"Sometimes we fly in the night before and fly out hours after a game. It just depends on our schedule. On this trip, we flew in the day before, had a night free, then had a morning skate before the game that night. As soon as the game was over, we flew out for our second game, went right to bed, had an optional morning skate, the game, and then came home after it ended."

"That sounds hectic. All the travel and they still expect you guys to be playing at your best."

"Just part of the game and you get used to it. Sleeping in a different hotel multiple nights a week becomes the norm. It makes home stretches all that more important. But on the flip side, we're not lacking in the amenities when we travel. We go on a private jet, so it isn't like we're crammed on a commercial flight."

"Must be nice." She smirks.

"I won't lie, there are definitely some perks that come with being a professional athlete, but they come with the demand of the job."

"I just never realized how much you are on the road."

"Every sport is different, so it's hard to compare. Take football, for instance. They play, what, seventeen games per season? We can play that many games in five, six weeks."

"That's crazy."

"Baseball also has a crazy long season, like we do, that requires lots of travel. They, however, tend to spend a few days in each city, playing three or four games against the same team before moving again."

"How much longer do you think you'll play?"

"That's the magical question. As many seasons as I can, but there are a lot of factors at play. I've got a few years left on my current contract. As long as I don't have any major injuries between now and then, I might retire once it expires, or I might try to land another small contract."

"If you were to get a new contract, would you want it with the Shockwaves?"

"That would be ideal. Moving teams is always a stressful time, especially coming into an established locker room. You have to be flexible enough to conform to their customs and the way they do things."

"Was being on a new team that hadn't already established those traditions harder than joining a team with them?"

"It was harder in the sense we had twenty-some-odd guys that all had their own thoughts, customs, and habits. We had to find a way to gel and find the chemistry athletes need in a team sport. Defensive players have to learn the quirks, strengths, and weaknesses of their line partners. Forwards have to learn what their linemates like to do in specific situations.

You get a line on the ice that has great chemistry, and they can pass the puck to one another without ever looking at the other player. They know exactly where the guy is going to be to hopefully make the play."

"I can see that," she says between bites.

"How was your week?" I ask.

"It was great. Ellie and I had a great time together. You have an amazing daughter."

"Thanks. I agree with you completely. Most of that is thanks to her mom. She's done the brunt of raising her."

"You don't give yourself enough credit," she says.

"The only part of my career that I regret is how much of Ellie's life I have missed. Michelle has always been great at keeping me informed on what's going on, but it still isn't the same as being there in person. I'm just lucky to have such a great kid. She's accepted our situation and rolled with the changes this year especially well."

"She has. I talked to her a little bit while you were gone about how she's doing. I could tell she missed her mom, but she also appreciates the opportunity to stay here, where she's always called home. She is, however, looking forward to her trip next month during fall break."

"I'm still a little shocked she decided to stay, if I'm being honest. I thought the first few weeks her mom was gone she'd decide that she didn't want to be away from her for that long."

"The stability of being able to stay at the same school and with her friends is important at her age and for the next few years."

"I can see that. I'm just happy it is all working out. I finally got out here, I'd hate for it to be for nothing."

"I pulled up the schedule for the season and don't see any conflicts as of now, so my offer still stands. If Ellie wants to stay with me, she's more than welcome to do so. I think it worked out well the last few days."

"I appreciate it, more than you can ever know. The little bit I've talked to her about it, she was happy with the arrangement."

"I think she enjoyed being able to sleep in her own bed at night, yet have someone to hang out with during the other times. Max sure enjoyed having another person around to give him head scratches."

"I'm glad it worked out all around, then," I say, chuckling as Max comes over to investigate what's going on with us after Avery said his name.

"What can I say, my dog loves everyone, but especially your daughter."

CHAPTER 14

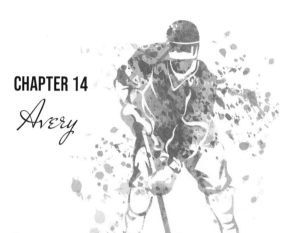

Avery

I WRAP a section of my hair around the flat iron, adding some volume and curls to it. I've already applied a very light amount of makeup, not wanting to go overboard before my date tonight with Ryker. I've felt straight-up giddy, today, as the hours ticked down until he told me he'd be ready.

I've still got about twenty-five minutes until then, so I've got plenty of time to finish with my hair. I settled on a pair of fitted jeans, ones that my best friend, Victoria, who goes by Tori, told me I had to buy. They have the distressed look, with manufactured holes on my thighs. They weren't my favorite, but I do have to agree, they look good. I paired them with a blouse that shows off a little more cleavage than I tend to, usually, but if I'm not going to show off on a date, what's the point in having cute clothes in my closet.

I carefully dance to the music I've got coming from my Bluetooth speaker in the bathroom. I don't want to accidentally burn myself, so I keep things to a minimum.

As I'm curling the last chunk of hair, all while "Girls Just Want to Have Fun" blares from the speaker, I hear a knock at my door. I look down at the time, and I still have ten minutes until Ryker is supposed to be here.

I put the flat iron down, and hit the button to shut my music off before running to the door. Max is already sitting next to it, ready to greet whoever is on the other side.

"Max, stay," I command before opening the door.

"Hi," Ryker greets. I do not miss the way his eyes travel down and back up my body. The heat in his eyes is scorching. If I were a sheet of ice, I'd be melting from that look alone. Instead, it is just my panties that are melting.

"Hi, come in," I greet, and take a step back so I can open the door all the way.

He steps in and instantly drops a hand to scratch the top of Max's head. "These are for you," he tells me, handing over a beautiful bouquet filled with all kinds of flowers.

"These are gorgeous, thank you," I tell him as I bring the flowers to my nose so I can get a good breath full of their scent. I take the vase to my table, setting them in the center.

"I know I was a few minutes early, so if you need to do anything before we leave, take your time."

"Let me just make sure my flat iron is off, and then I'll feed Max quick, and we can get out of here."

"No problem," he states, moving further into my living room. I watch as he takes a seat and Max follows him to the couch, where he sits at Ryker's feet, loving all the attention Ryker is bestowing on him. I pull my eyes from them and hurry to my bathroom, unplugging my flat iron and giving myself a once-over in the mirror. Satisfied I'm as put together as I'm going to be, I flick off the light and head back to the living room.

I quickly measure out Max's dinner, placing the bowl in his kennel where he's accustomed to eating all of his meals. At the sound of his bowl hitting the plastic bottom, he heads straight to it and starts chomping down.

"Shall we?" I ask, getting Ryker's attention.

"We shall," he agrees as he stands and follows me to the door.

"So, where exactly are we going tonight?" I ask, since he's given me very little insight into our date tonight.

"We have reservations at Seven Hills. I hope you like Italian food, as it was recommended to me as one of the best Italian places in San Francisco."

"I love Italian food, and I've heard amazing things about the place, I've just never been, myself."

"Well then, I guess we get to experience it for the first time together," Ryker says as he escorts me to the elevator. The doors open immediately after he presses the down button. He places his hand on my lower back as we both step through the doors. The heat of his fingers, even through my clothes, is like a branding on my skin. I can feel him everywhere and he's hardly touched me yet.

"I didn't tell you before, but you look beautiful tonight," Ryker says, just before the elevator doors open into the garage.

"Thank you," I tell him as I blush from his compliment. "You look pretty sharp, yourself," I tell him as I look him up and down. He's got on a polo and a pair of jeans that hug his thick thighs perfectly. I can only imagine how hard it is for him to find clothes that fit him, with the amount of muscle he's got.

"You're welcome," he says as he leads me over to his car. Ever the gentleman, he opens my door, and waits for me to get in before he shuts it and makes his way around the front of the car before opening and getting into the driver's seat.

"This is a nice car," I say, looking around as I sink lower into the seat. The leather is like butter underneath me.

"One thing I've always splurged on since going pro is having a nice car."

"Nothing wrong with that," I tell him.

"Some guys like to spend their money on a huge house or outdoor toys, or even extravagant vacations. Not me. I'd rather spend it on a nice car I can use year-round."

"At least you know what you like."

"What do you like to splurge on for yourself?" he asks as we pull out onto the road.

"Hmm..." I hum, thinking about the question. "I've never legitimately splurged on something big. Maybe a couple of trips to the spa each year. I love going and getting massages, especially with the amount of time I spend sitting at a computer desk, hunched over."

"Massages are a great way to relax. I see our therapist weekly, sometimes daily if I'm nursing an injury or some tight muscles."

"Does the team have a massage therapist on staff?" I ask.

"A couple of them. Plus, the physical therapist can also do some massage if we're working on a specific area. When they do the massage, it isn't usually as relaxing, as they're digging into the muscle, which can actually be quite painful."

"Sounds painful," I agree.

We make small talk the rest of the way to the restaurant. After circling twice, looking for a parking spot, Ryker gives up and just pulls over to the valet stand outside the restaurant. Both of our doors are opened at the same time.

"Holy crap, you're Ryker Jorgensen," the valet on his side says when Ryker steps out.

"Sure am. Are you a fan?" he asks the young man.

"Just started watching hockey with the new team playing here, so I'm still learning," he tells him.

"Thanks for the support. Have you made it to a game, yet?" Ryker asks him.

"Not yet. I hope to save up enough to get a ticket to a game."

"If you had a ticket, could you make it to the next home game?"

"Maybe," the guy answers, a confused look on his face. "When is it?" he asks.

"Sunday at four," Ryker states.

"Yeah, I'm off that day," he tells Ryker.

"Tell you what. You give me your name and I'll have two tickets waiting for you at will call for Sunday's game."

"Are you serious?" the guy says, a little shocked.

"Absolutely!" Ryker assures him.

The guy writes out his name on a claim ticket and hands it to Ryker.

"Maybe add your cell number so they can reach you, if needed," Ryker says, handing the ticket back to the guy. He writes out the number and hands it back to him.

"Thank you so much. I'm speechless and don't know what else to say."

"No need for anything else, just go and have a

good time," Ryker tells him. He hands him a tip and takes the claim slip for the keys.

"Thank you. I sure will," he tells us before Ryker joins me on the passenger side of the car. His hand lands on my lower back like earlier, only, this time, he's a few inches closer to me. My shoulder pressed against his as we walked together into the restaurant.

"That was sweet of you," I tell him as we go.

"Happy to do it. We're given an allotment of tickets we can give away, and this seemed like a good time to use that perk," he tells me. We approach the hostess stand, and before Ryker can give them his name, an older gentleman recognizes him.

"Mr. Jorgensen, thank you for dining with us this evening. If you're ready to be seated, I can take you directly to your table."

"Thank you. We're looking forward to it. I've heard it's the best Italian place in the entire city."

"We take pride in being labeled the best," the man says as he stops at a table for two that is tucked in a little nook. I look around and realize they have an entire wall of nooks, with small tables placed in each of them, giving each party a little bit of privacy. "Your server will be here shortly. The first two pages are our drink menu, followed by the appetizer list, and finally, the main courses."

"Thanks," Ryker tells him before he steps away. "Do you like wine?" he asks.

"Occasionally, but it isn't my go-to drink," I tell him.

"Me, either, but I was willing to split a bottle with you, if you wanted one."

"I'd prefer the cocktail menu," I assure him. He smirks, and I'm sure his mind went straight to the gutter at the word cock, and I can't help but look up at him with my own sexy smirk.

"Ms. Reid, you are a little vixen, aren't you?"

"I guess you'll have to find out," I flirt back.

Ryker's smile could melt panties right off a woman. I'm spared when our server approaches our table.

"Good evening, and welcome to Seven Hills. I'm April and I'll be serving you tonight. Can I start you off with some drinks and an appetizer?"

"I'll do a lemon drop martini," I tell her before I look back at Ryker. We hadn't had time to discuss an appetizer, yet.

"I'll try your IPA," he tells her. "And can you give us a minute on food, we haven't decided just yet."

"Of course, take your time. I'll go get your drinks and be back." She steps away and Ryker and I both turn back to our menus.

"What are you thinking?" I ask him. So many things sound amazing, it is hard to decide on just one option.

"The garlic and parmesan focaccia sounds good," he suggests.

"I was thinking the same thing," I tell him.

"What are you thinking for dinner?"

"I'm trying to decide between the market fish and the New York strip."

"We could each order one and share them. Both sound good to me," he suggests.

"Are you sure? I don't want you ordering something you don't want."

"I was leaning toward the steak, myself."

"Perfect, then you order the steak, and I'll get the fish."

"How do you like your steak cooked?" he asks.

"Medium, usually, but it's your meal, order it however you like."

"You're in luck, I also like mine medium." He winks at me. "We have more and more in common the longer we spend time together."

"I think we're playing right into Ellie's plans."

"Thank you for your help with her. I can't thank you enough for stepping in, especially last-minute this past week."

"It was no hardship. I truly enjoyed spending time with her and getting to know her better. She genuinely is a great kid."

April returns with our drinks, she takes our order and menus, and leaves us to our conversation. I feel so comfortable and at ease with Ryker. I love seeing all the different sides of him. The way he is with his daughter, the professional athlete that is willing to give his time to talk with a new fan and give him something without ever being asked, and now the relaxed and flirty version. Besides his dad side, this is my favorite. It might be because his attention is directed my way, which I'm not complaining about one bit.

CHAPTER 15
Ryker

AVERY and I finish up our dinner. The sexual tension between us built with every bite of food we fed each other. I thought my dick was going to bust the seam of my jeans when she looked directly into my eyes while wrapping her lips around the fork, accepting a bite of steak I fed her. I had to clear my throat, seconds later, to help clear my mind of the visuals that were flashing on what other things she could wrap those lips around.

"Can I interest you in some dessert?" April asks as she clears our dinner plates from the table.

"I'm so full, I don't think I can eat another bite, right now," Avery tells her.

"Of course. You want another round of drinks, or should I bring the check?" April asks me.

"The check, please," I tell her as I fish my wallet

out of my back pocket. I hand her my card before she can even leave the table.

"I'll be right back," she assures us.

"So, what's next?" Avery asks.

"Did you want to walk around, some? I've never been down here so I'm not sure what the area has to offer," I tell her.

"Sure. I haven't been down in this area in years, so I'm sure it has changed some."

April returns with my card and the receipt for me to sign. I add a generous tip and sign my name. "Thanks, it was great tonight," I tell her before we stand to leave.

"Thanks for dining with us," she states. I offer Avery my hand as she stands from her seat. I take advantage of her hand in mine, and link our fingers together as we walk out of the restaurant. The valet guys see us right away and head in our direction.

"Are you ready for your car, Mr. Jorgensen?"

"Actually, I think we're going to go walk around for a little bit. Is it okay if we leave it here?"

"Of course. We're open until eleven, so you're good until then."

"Perfect. I don't think we'll be out that late, but good to know anyhow."

We walk a few blocks until we can see the water. The sun has set, so the area is only illuminated by the street and building lights. "I bet the sunsets are amazing down here by the water," I say.

"They are. I used to come down here often to watch them, especially in the summertime."

"You don't anymore?" I ask as we stop in a bump-out area people can look out at the water. The moon is big and bright as it reflects off the water.

"I haven't in a while. I used to come down with my ex, mostly, and after we broke up, it felt kind of weird to come by myself. Plus, it can sometimes not be the safest place for a woman to be hanging around by herself. I'm pretty content just staying home these days, to be honest. Don't get me wrong, I enjoy getting out every once in a while, but I'm also good with sticking close to home."

"I can understand that. When I'm able to be home, I do the same. I do enough traveling during the season, so I'm not sad about not seeing the inside of a hotel room during our off time, if I don't have to. I put up with it to take Ellie on a trip or two, but it's different since I'm getting time with her."

"I'm sure she loves just getting to spend time with you, no matter where it is at."

"That she is, and I imagine it will be the same, now, with Michelle. Has she said anything more to you about missing her mom, or regretting her decision to stay here?"

"Nope. Just how excited she was to see her in a few weeks."

"I guess I hit the lottery when it came to Ellie."

"You sure did. Have you ever wanted more kids?" Avery asks.

"Not really. I've never even considered settling down with someone, as I haven't had any serious relationships. Most women don't want to deal with my demanding schedule, or the fact all of my off time was dedicated to being with Ellie. Not to stereotype your gender, but women can get kind of jealous, and I'm not up for dealing with a jealous woman. My daughter is my priority, and if someone isn't okay with that, then they aren't worth my time. I don't ever want her to feel like she isn't a priority. Especially all the years leading up to now. My time with her was limited and I savored every moment I got with her."

"I can tell you honestly, you've accomplished it. She couldn't be prouder of you. She understands the constraints and demands of your job and doesn't hold it against you. She might only be fifteen, but she's so much more mature than her actual age."

"Thank you for that. I always fear I'm letting her down in one way or another."

"The way she talks about you tells a completely different story, so I don't think you've got anything to worry about."

"What about you, do you want kids?" I ask, turning Avery's question back on her.

"I do, but I'm also not going to force it. If I'm

meant to be a mom, it will happen when it's supposed to. The same goes with meeting my soul mate and falling in love, living together, getting married—all of that."

"You're refreshing, has anyone ever told you that?" I ask. Avery turns so we're facing one another, and I can't help but want to be as close to her as I can, so I close the few-inch gap between us. I pull her close, her hands slipping around my torso as mine cup her cheeks.

"No," she whispers as she looks up at me. I lower my head slowly. My intent is clear, I'm going to kiss her unless she stops me.

"Please don't hurt me," she whispers just before our lips connect. Her words hit me, and I wonder what her ex did to her for her to say that to me. It irritates me someone could have hurt her. But it also gives me the desire to erase every bad memory she has and replace them with only good memories.

I deepen the kiss, swiping my tongue along the seam of her lips. She opens instantly for me, the sour from her lemon drop martini a faint taste against my own tastebuds. I kiss her until I don't know where I end and she begins. Breaking our connection, I rest my forehead against hers and suck in a much-needed breath.

"Ready to get out of here?" I ask.

"So ready," she agrees.

I don't need to be told twice. I drop a quick kiss on her lips, wanting one last taste of them to hold me over until we're back home. I grab her hand, linking them together as we walk back to the valet stand to get my car.

"Did you want to stop for dessert anywhere?" I ask once we're back on the road.

"No, I'm good. I probably have some ice cream in the freezer if we get hungry later," Avery says. I move my gaze to her, for a moment, the desire is practically rolling off of her, the way she's looking at me.

I can't help but smirk. If things go how I hope they do, we're both going to need to refuel later.

"Don't say I didn't offer," I tell her as I squeeze her thigh, slipping two fingers inside one of the holes lining her thighs in her torn jeans. I've wondered many times tonight what her skin would feel like against mine. She's smooth and it fuels my desire to feel more of her. The flashes of her cleavage have had my hands craving the feeling of what it will be like to cradle them, flicking her nipples to see how long it takes to have her crying out in need.

"You can have me for dessert," she says, and I almost swerve.

"Fuck, Avery." I groan. "You can't say things like that while I'm driving if you want to make it home in one piece."

"Sorry, not sorry." She smirks. "Just laying it out there, in case I wasn't sending you the right signals."

"Oh, you're sending signals," I tell her as the GPS instructs me to get over for the exit we're approaching.

It doesn't take long for us to reach the condo building. I park quickly, not bothering to make sure I'm perfectly centered. I just want to get this beautiful woman upstairs and in bed as quickly as possible.

"You're place or mine?" I ask Avery once we're in the elevator. I've backed her up against the wall, ready to kiss her again, but holding back as the ride up isn't a long one.

"If we go to mine, I'll have to deal with Max, first, so your place will be distraction-free."

"Then, my place it is," I tell her as the bell dings when the doors open. I quickly snatch her hand, pulling her swiftly down the hall. Avery stumbles trying to keep up with my long strides.

"In a hurry for something?" she asks as we come to a stop outside my door.

"Yep, my dessert." I smirk at her, my eyes smoldering as they bore into hers.

Avery licks her lips and it's my undoing. I slide my key into the deadbolt, turning it so I can open the door. I hold it so she can walk in before me, giving myself a couple of seconds to take in a few calming breaths. I don't want to rush this. I want to savor it.

"You good?" Avery asks.

"Of course, why?" I ask.

"You went a little quiet and looked like you were second-guessing this," she says, motioning between the two of us.

I reach for her, pulling her back into my arms. "Quite the opposite. I was willing my body to slow down. I don't want to rush anything with you. I want to savor you, this moment. I don't know what it is about you, but you make me feel like there could be more. Like I can have it all, the career, my daughter, and a relationship."

"Ryker," Avery says my name as she tugs my face down to hers, "kiss me and take me to bed."

I don't have to be told twice. I kiss her hard and lift her up until my hands are cradling her ass and her legs wrap around my waist.

I break our kiss, only to carry her back to my room. I don't need either of us getting injured before we can strip. I push through my door, slamming it shut behind me. No taking chances Ellie changes her plans and comes home tonight and finds us having sex. I don't need that awkward situation happening at any time.

Avery slides down my front and guides my hands up her torso, slipping them underneath her shirt. If I thought touching her thigh in the car was heaven, having both of my hands on her skin is nirvana. She tugs me down until our lips meet again. I quite enjoy her taking the lead, so I let Avery set the pace. She licks her way inside my mouth as my hands explore her body as much as they can within the confines of her shirt. I slip my thumbs over the lace front of her bra, finding her nipples already turning to pebbled buds.

I break the kiss and pull her shirt off over her head. I get my first full look at her tits. They look to be a perfect size, a little more than a handful. I unclasp her bra, letting it fall to the floor before I cup them in my hands. I rub her dusty pink nipples, making them pebble even harder. "Ryker." She gasps my name when I drop my mouth to one of those perky nipples, sucking and flicking it with my tongue. Her gasps have me wondering just how my name on her lips will sound when I first slide into her and then when I made her come on my cock.

Her moans are the encouragement I need as I tease her. Avery slides her hands into my hair, holding me tightly to her chest as if she doesn't want me to ever leave this position. I'm all for that, except for the fact I have another desire, to taste her between her thighs.

Releasing her breast with a pop, I look up and capture her kiss-swollen lips with mine. "You're a little overdressed," she says mid-kiss, so I reach behind my head and tug my polo shirt off. We're both topless, now, but I don't stop there. I unbutton my jeans and push them down. I sit on the edge of the bed so I can tug them off my legs without falling.

With only my boxer briefs on, I grip my aching cock. *It's almost your turn, buddy,* I mentally think and tell my dick.

Looking up at Avery, she's watching my every move. Her eyes are a little wide as she watches my hand move over my crotch. I grab her hand and pull her between my thighs as I sit on the edge of the bed. "Like what you see?" I ask as she places her palms on my chest.

"You're like a chiseled slab of stone, your muscles have muscles," she says, moving her hands around my torso before looking down at her own body.

I can see the worry in her eyes, and I want none of it. "Talk to me," I plead as she pulls her hands from my chest and attempts to cover her own body up.

"This might have been a bad idea," she says, looking very nervous.

"Avery," I say her name, probably a little sharper than I intended, but it gets her attention. "You are beautiful," I tell her as I grab for her hands. She allows me to hold them in mine, so I'm taking that as a win. "Your body is perfect just the way it is. You aren't meant to be muscular like I am. I need to be like this to be the best I can be at my job. I'll be honest, I probably wouldn't be as attracted to you if you did look like me. I like you soft and smooth," I tell her as I let go of one of her hands so I can slide my fingertips down her belly. She's soft but trim, but not in a "I work out for five hours a day" way, more the "I care about my body and eat healthily, but still enjoy a cookie every now and then" way.

"You're sure? I know with your status, you could have any woman you want, the fitness-focused type, or some Barbie doll look-alike," she says nervously.

"Avery, those types of women have never appealed to me. I want someone real. Someone I can laugh with, cuddle on the couch and share a bowl of ice cream with, and then take to bed and ravish all night long. I want the morning breath moments as much as I want someone I can get dressed up with and head to the team's charity event. Don't ever think you need to compete with any other woman for my attention. Is that something that might interest you?" I ask, trying to be as real with her as I can.

"You make it so easy to want the same," she says, running her fingers through my hair again.

"Then, let me show you just how good it can be, how much you turn me on."

Avery steps back, and I worry for a second she's going to grab her clothes and bolt out the door. Instead, she unbuttons her jeans, sliding them down her hips and legs until she's standing in front of me in only her panties. "Leave them," I instruct. "Let me take them off." She does as requested and leaves the small scrap of fabric covering the most intimate parts of her body. Ones I won't take for granted being given access to. "Come, lay down," I suggest, patting the bed.

I watch as Avery sits down, sliding until she's lying in the center of my big bed, her head on one of the pillows, her body on display for my eyes only.

"You're so fucking gorgeous," I tell her before I descend, giving in to what we both so badly want and need.

"Ryker." She cries out my name when I nip at the sensitive skin of her inner thighs. I still haven't touched her center, which has taken every ounce of self-control I possess.

"Yes, babe?" I press a kiss to her mound.

"More, I need more," she tells me.

"Where do you need more?" I ask, purposely being obtuse.

"You know damn well where I need more." She pushes her upper body up, so she's propped on her elbows, and stares me down. I can't help but laugh at her trying to be mad, all while my mouth is inches from the exact spot she wants it.

"How about here?" I ask, circling her clit through her panties.

"Ye-yes," she pants as I circle faster.

"And how about this?" I ask, moving the fabric to the side so I can lick her seam. Her body trembles at my touch. My dick responds by hardening as it presses against the mattress. I can feel pre-cum leaking from my tip in anticipation of what's happening. I stop and pull her panties completely off her body. I no longer need or want them in my way.

With the fabric out of my way, I return my fingers to her clit. "Oh, yes." I hear the words fall from her lips. Encouraged by her reaction, I replace my fingers circling her clit with my tongue. I tease her, alternating between sucking her clit hard and flicking it with my tongue. I can tell she's close by the way her thighs start to clench around my head, pinning me in place. I slide two fingers inside her opening, quickly finding her sweet spot from the inside. I clamp down on her clit, sucking it hard into my mouth as I fuck her with my fingers. That's all it takes, and her body goes completely rigid as it bows off the bed. I don't let up, wanting her to experience every possible second of her orgasm. My fingers, slick with her release, the sweetness hitting my tongue as I lick at her clit as it pulses with her release.

As her body relaxes into the mattress, her orgasm waning, I slow my thrusts and licks. Moving to kiss her thighs once more, then her belly as I make my way up the bed. I nip and suck at the underside of her tits, loving the way her body responds to my touch.

"How are you feeling, now?" I ask once I reach the pillow and can lie down next to her.

"Languid, and like I'm on a cloud," she says, snuggling into my side.

"Good," I chuckle, accomplishing what I was

after. "You let me know when you're ready for round two and I'll make you come on my cock, next."

"I've never come more than once," she whispers in her blissed-out state.

"I'm going to change that," I tell her adamantly.

"Someone's confident." She chuckles.

"Damn straight, woman," I tell her as I smack her ass, grabbing a handful of it as I pull us closer.

We lay for a few minutes in complete silence, the only noises in the room coming from our breathing. Avery stirs, her hand snaking down my body until she's gripping my cock. "Fuck," I hiss at the contact.

"You should take these off," she tells me, snapping the elastic band of my underwear. I quickly lift my hips, shoving them down and using my feet to kick them the rest of the way off my body and onto the floor.

"Better?" I ask, her hand already back on my cock.

"Mhmm," she hums, and before I can do anything about it, she's slid down my body and has my cock in her mouth.

"Holy shit," I moan as my tip hits the back of her throat. The vixen moans and the vibrations tickle my tip. I want so bad to thrust my hips up, but use every ounce of control to keep them pinned to the mattress and let her keep control of this.

I look down, just as she pops my tip from her lips, everything glistening from the wetness, and I want nothing more than for her pussy to be gripping my cock. "Ride me," I suggest.

"Do you have a condom close by?" she asks, and I can't believe I didn't think of one, first. I'm always so careful when I do have sex, but she has me completely wrapped up in her, I didn't this time.

"Yeah," I tell her as I push up and lean over to my nightstand. I open the drawer and pull out a box. Tearing it open, I grab out a few, tossing the extras on the nightstand for easy access. Holding one up between my fingers, I ask, "Do you want the honors or should I?"

"You can," she says, and proceeds to watch as I rip the packet open, then roll it down my shaft. I help her get situated, straddling my lap. Her wet pussy sits just below my shaft, close enough I can feel her heat. I slide a hand behind her neck, pulling her down to meet me. "Ride me until you come," I instruct, kissing her tenderly for a moment before deepening the kiss.

She pulls back, breaking our connection, and I almost protest, but stop the moment she lifts her body and aligns her opening with my tip and then slowly slides down my length. "Oh," she moans. "I feel so full," she tells me as she settles herself with her hands on my chest. I want to pound into her so fucking bad, but I hold still, letting her adjust for as long as she needs to. From what I gather from our conversation, it has been a little while since her last time, so her body needs to adjust.

I place my hands on her hips, ready to help her move when she's ready. Avery slowly pushes up, lifting until just the tip is still inside, then drops down, faster than I anticipated her to do, at first. My body is ready for go time, so I have to bite back my own urge to empty my release inside her. Her rhythm picks up, her thrusts becoming quite fast as she pistons up and down. "That's it, baby, chase your release," I grit out. I can feel my body is ready to come, but I bite it back, wanting to show Avery she can come multiple times in one night.

"I can't get there," she pants, her movements slowing as she starts to tire out. I wrap my arms around her back and flip us in one movement, never breaking our connection.

"I'll get you there," I tell her, kissing her deeply before I pull out and adjust our position one more time. I tug her to the edge of the bed and place her heels up on my shoulders. I slide my cock back inside her, the position creating an all-new tightness and feeling for both of us.

"Oh my god," she cries as I start to thrust. My balls tingle with my release. I swivel my hips, trying to find the perfect spot that will make her explode. I can feel her muscles as they start to flutter, the telltale sign her orgasm is building. "Ryker, yes, please don't stop," she cries. I watch as pure euphoria takes hold of her body. I slam my cock inside her as hard as I can possibly thrust, my headboard cracking against the wall. If I'm not careful, I'll crack it with the force.

"That's it, baby, come for me." I coach her until her pussy is clamping down like a vise grip on my length. I let go, allowing myself to fall over the crest as the explosive currents of my own orgasm flow from my body. "Shit, that was perfect," I say between breaths.

Avery's legs fall to my sides as I collapse forward. I do my best to keep the majority of my weight off of her as I lean into my forearms on the bed. Her nails scape up and down my back, almost light enough to feel like a tickling sensation. She hits one specific spot and my cock pulses in response.

"I need a break before I can go again." She giggles.

"Babe, I need a nap before I can even think straight again," I tell her as I push up enough so I can kiss her.

"You were determined to make me come multiple times," she says when we end our kiss.

"I told you I could make it happen." I wink at her. "And if you stay the night, I can do it at least one more time."

"Is that an invitation?" she asks.

"Yes, definitely an invitation. Unless we should stay at your place, so Max isn't alone."

"That might not be a bad idea. I at least need to

go home and let him out. He's probably in need of a bathroom break by now."

I pull out, immediately missing the feeling of being buried deep inside Avery. But I know I'll be back inside her, if I have my way, and that will be in only a few more hours.

CHAPTER 16

Avery

I FALL BACK on my couch. My legs are killing me after the four-mile walk I just took Max out on. I was feeling a little guilty about how much I've left him alone lately, so we took an extra-long walk today. My cell rings, and I look down to see Tori calling, so I quickly answer.

"Hello, about time you call me," I greet.

"I'm so sorry. Our contact with the outside world was so limited, and when we did have the ability to email or text, we usually kept it to checking in with the humanitarian organization," she apologizes.

"Tell me all about it, was it amazing?" I ask.

"Avery, I can't even describe what we saw while there. It was beautiful, but also heartbreaking. Some of the villages we came upon were sometimes just a few shacks, no more than what many back home would consider a treehouse for kids to play in, yet these people lived there. The poverty was hard to get over. I wanted to help every single person we came into contact with but knew I couldn't."

"That does sound heartbreaking and hard to internalize. Were you able to bring aide to as many places as you'd hoped?" I asked. My best friend had been away on a six-week humanitarian trip in Africa. Her employer was a major donor to the cause and had the opportunity to send volunteers to help with taking supplies to areas in need. Be it food and water to basic medical supplies, they collected, sorted, shipped, and then distributed it all out.

"I think so. We successfully distributed every-thing we set out to take, so that's a good thing. We also successfully made it out without anyone from our team getting hurt or having any major problems. We had one flat tire along the way, but a couple of the guys got it taken care of fairly quickly."

"That's good. I'm so glad you're back. Have you had time to decompress since returning or do I have to wait even longer to see you?" I ask.

"Someone's impatient." She laughs into the phone.

"No, I just miss my best friend and have so much to tell you about," I say, already feeling giddy telling her about Ryker. I can't wait to introduce them and get her opinion on my sexy next-door neighbor/new man crush, or possibly boyfriend? We haven't specifically had the conversation, yet, but I think after the last two nights together, it is on the horizon.

"What did I miss?" she asks, perking up. I can just picture the inquisitive look on her face at this moment in time.

"So, do you remember how I told you I have a hunky new neighbor who bought Ruth's place?"

"Yeah, the athlete, right?" she asks.

"Yep, hockey player," I tell her. "I've gotten to know Ryker and his daughter Ellie pretty well the last few weeks, like, really-*really* well."

"You didn't," she squeals. "Tell me everything. Does he have a big dick? And better yet, does he know how to use it?" she asks.

"What, it's only about the sex?" I ask her, pretending to be offended.

"Honey, we're not getting any younger, so yes, it's about the sex. There's no sense in settling if the sex isn't incredible."

"Well, it's a good thing the sex is incredible, then," I tell her. I sigh as I think back on the last two nights Ryker and I have spent together.

"You go, girl! I'm so jealous. Does he have any single friends or teammates?"

I can't help but laugh at her question. "I'm sure he does. I haven't met anyone on his team, and we haven't talked much about them. Just some basics on what it's been like to be on a brand-new team and how they've handled having so many opinions on how they do things, making their own traditions to pass down in years to come."

"So, I take it there isn't much talking, just sexy times?" she says.

"No," I laugh. "We've only had the sexy times this weekend. Most of the time, we're around each other when his daughter is home. I've actually spent more time with just Ellie than I have with Ryker," I tell her.

"Why's that?"

"He's still figuring out who she'll stay with or will stay with her when he's on the road. She was supposed to go stay at her best friend's house for his first road trip of the season, but those arrangements fell through last minute when her friend's family all came down with the flu, so I offered to stay with her. It was a win-win situation, as we both got to sleep in our own beds but had someone to hang out with in the evenings. She's truly a sweet kid, so it wasn't a hardship, at all," I tell Tori. "I actually offered to do it for all of his trips. He still hasn't fully agreed because he feels like he's taking advantage, but it isn't like I'm not just next door to him already."

"Are you officially dating?" she asks. "Or just got a next-door neighbor with benefits thing going on?"

"We haven't labeled anything, but if I was a gambling person, I'd bet we'll have an official conversation with labels, sooner than later."

"Maybe he'll feel better with you helping out

with Ellie if you guys are a couple, so maybe just wait until then to broach the conversation," she suggests.

"I'm not super worried about it, my offer is out there. Ellie liked the arrangement and not having to leave home. I can see Ryker letting Ellie make the final decision, so I think we'll be fine."

"I leave for two months and your life completely changes," she huffs.

"I'll get you all caught up, I promise. Now, when can I see you?"

"In about two minutes," she says.

"What?!" I screech. "You're here?"

"Yep, just pulling into your parking lot now!"

I run to my door, pulling it open so I can meet her at the top of the elevator, but instead of an empty hallway, I run straight into a hard chest.

"Where are you off to?" Ryker asks, an amused tone lacing his voice. He places his hands on my arms, steadying me so I don't fall.

"Tori is back! She'll be up any second now," I tell him just as the elevator doors open.

It's like a chick-flick, when two long-lost friends see one another for the first time after a long time apart. We both run toward each other, meeting in the middle in a massive hug.

"I'm so happy you're home!" I squeeze my best friend as we walk to my door, the one Ryker is leaning against the jam of.

"You must be Ryker. I'm Victoria, but please, call me Tori."

"Nice to meet you, Tori. I am, in fact, Ryker," he greets her, holding a hand out for her to shake.

"I've heard all about you in the last thirty minutes," Tori tells him.

"And I learned all about you the other night at dinner," he tells her.

"If it was anything bad, don't believe it. I was the good one, so don't let her tell you anything different." Tori tries to play off as the innocent friend. I don't think Ryker is buying her bullshit, as he shouldn't.

"Um, yeah, I don't think so. Who was the one to get expelled from school?" I ask, reminding her just how bad she was in high school.

"Yeah, yeah, okay, so I was the bad influence, but I've grown up and changed. Those days are behind me," she insists.

"Hey, we were all young and dumb once," Ryker states.

"Not this one," Tori says, pointing at me. "She was the good one. Never wanting to do anything that could possibly get her into trouble. She was the good angel on my shoulder, keeping me from getting into more trouble than I already was."

"We all need a friend like that," he says.

"I guess so. I'd probably be living a much

different life if Avery didn't keep me on the straight and narrow."

"I don't mean to rush, but I've got to head to the rink. I was just stopping over to make sure you were still able to bring Ellie later?" he asks.

"Of course. We'll be there, cheering loud," I assure him.

"Perfect. She's working on some homework, but will be ready around two thirty or three."

"Do you think there's a chance of getting a third ticket?" I ask, wondering if it would be okay to invite Tori to come.

"Possibly. Let me send a text to find out and I'll let you know, sound good?"

"Perfect," I tell him. I can tell he isn't sure what our exchange should be, at this point, especially with Tori watching our exchange, so I make the decision for him when I push up on my toes and kiss him. He pulls me closer, deepening the kiss, yet still managing to keep it mostly PG.

"It was nice to meet you, Ryker. I'm sure we'll be seeing lots of each other now that I'm back in the States."

"Nice meeting you, Tori. I look forward to it," he tells her before giving me one last chaste kiss and heading back out the door.

I look over and Max has finally decided to move his sleepy butt and greet Tori. She's sat down on the floor and is letting him attack her with kisses all over her face. "Don't let him go too crazy," I remind her. "I don't want him greeting everyone like that."

"Who's a good boy?" she asks him. "Has your mom been neglecting you while I've been gone?" she asks him as he happily wags his tail as she pushes him back from kissing her face.

"I have definitely not been neglecting him. Hell, we got back from a four-mile walk just before you called. He's still the spoiled dog he was before you left," I assure her.

"And what about all the extra time you've been spending next door?" she asks, her eyebrows raising in question at me.

"Not all of that time has been at his place," I tell her, and can feel my cheeks go red with my embarrassment. I've never felt super comfortable talking about sex with others, especially my sex life. I'm usually of the mindset that what happens between two partners should stay between the two of them. Sex is very personal and isn't something everyone needs to know the details about, so I stay pretty quiet on the topic.

"You go, girl! I hope that man breaks you out of your shell. You deserve it."

"I don't know about deserving it, but he's been good for my confidence," I tell her.

"Hell yes, he has! Any man would be lucky to call you his, Ryker included."

"If you say so," I try and brush off her compliment.

"Stop that shit, Avery. You are more than worthy of any standup guy's attention and love. I've only been around the guy for a few minutes, but I saw the way he looked at you, the way he waited for you to make the move to show any PDA before he initiated anything further. I didn't miss the fact he wanted to take things further but held back because he could sense you were uncomfortable with it in front of people."

"You picked up on all of that in those five minutes?" I ask, a little shocked.

"Yep, that man is a goner for you. And, from what I can tell, is one of the good ones. Do whatever you can to keep him. I'm telling you, now, he's your future."

"I don't know how you can get all that out of such a short interaction."

"It was an immediate gut feeling," she tells me.

"If you say so," I concede. "I hope he can get you a ticket. I'll feel bad if I have to ditch you, but I did commit to taking Ellie to today's game."

"If he can't, we can get together tomorrow, or later this week," she assures me.

I pull my best friend into a hug. I can't believe she's finally home. I've missed her so damn much. I didn't realize how much I'd turned into a hermit while she was gone. Well, that is, until Ryker and Ellie came into my life.

"I've missed you so damn much. I'm glad you had a good trip, but also glad you're home, now," I tell her honestly.

"Feeling's mutual. I wouldn't trade anything in the world for my experience as a volunteer, but I'm not jumping at the chance to do another long trip again. It did, however, bring into perspective just how lucky we are in life, not having to worry about our next meal, or having access to clean drinking water. I have a brand new perspective on life. A new desire to help those who are less fortunate than we are. I want to find a shelter or food bank to start volunteering with. Even if I can only afford to donate my time, it is better than nothing."

"When you find a place, sign me up to go with you. Depending on when it is, Ellie might want to join us. She was telling me about a program at school where she gets credit for when she volunteers, so it might be something she's interested in."

"I'll keep it in mind when searching," Tori states.

My cell dings, alerting me to my incoming text message. I find my phone as I'd apparently set it down on the couch after coming back inside.

RYKER

Ticket has been secured; it should be in your app shortly.

> Thank you so much! I owe you something. {Smiley winky face}

I'll take sexual favors.

> Duh.

Glad we're on the same page, however, let's bookmark this conversation for later tonight. I just got to the rink and don't need a hard-on while trying to warm up for the game. That will make stretching awkward, especially if one of the strength and conditioning coaches helps me stretch out today.

> Got it, have a good game. We'll see you after.

Sounds good.

I toss my phone back on the couch, a smile tugging at my lips.

"Let me guess, lover boy?" Tori asks.

"Yeah. Oh and he got you a ticket, so get ready for your first hockey game," I tell her.

"Are you serious?" she asks. "I know nothing about hockey."

"That's okay, I don't understand much, either, but Ellie will be with us, and she can explain it all to us.

She's been helping me learn when we watch together."

"Okay, should I run home, first? Do I need to change?" she asks, looking down at her jeans and T-shirt.

"You should be fine. You can borrow a sweatshirt, as the rink can be chilly."

"I'm so excited!" she cheers. We're interrupted by a knock at the door.

"Hey, Ellie, did you get your assignment done?" I ask after she walks in.

"Yep, just finished up a little bit ago."

"Good. Hey, I wanted to introduce you to my best friend, Tori," I say, leading her into my condo. "Tori, this is Ellie," I introduce and they give each other a little wave.

"Nice to meet you," Tori tells her.

"Likewise. Have you been here long? Avery was telling me a little bit about your trip and that you'd be home soon."

"I got back early yesterday but slept for, like, sixteen hours straight after making it home. I came over here as soon as I was up and showered."

"Have you eaten?" I ask, not realizing she came straight here.

"I stopped and grabbed something quick on the drive over. I didn't realize just how much I missed the convenience of a drive through."

"I'm still shocked you survived without Starbucks for so long. Did you almost kill anyone with withdrawals?"

"Funny," she deadpans. "They had coffee. It wasn't my normal, but kept me caffeinated, at least. The first airport we got to that had a Starbucks in it was like heaven. I had two drinks before it was time to board the flight. Then, I spent the next four hours going back and forth to the bathroom."

"That's no fun," Ellie replies.

"Oh, it wasn't any digestive issues, I'd just drank so much so fast that I kept having to pee." Tori laughs.

"Well, it's better, but still, those airplane bathrooms aren't all that easy to use. I swear, they make them smaller and smaller each time I fly."

"You aren't wrong there," Tori agrees with her.

"So, your dad was able to get us one more ticket so Tori can come with us to the game. You'll have to roll back the hockey 101 class you've been giving me to bring her up to speed, as she's also a hockey virgin."

"Awesome. I can tell you all about the sport. It's pretty fun when you get into it."

"Cool, I look forward to it," Tori tells her.

"When did you want to head out?" I ask Ellie.

"I'm ready whenever you are. Puck drop is at four, today, so do you want to head out around two thirty?"

"That should give us time to get parked and

inside the rink, even with enough time so Tori can see warmups."

"We can go down to the boards and watch them up close," Ellie suggests.

"That would be fun," I agree.

"I'll run back home and grab my stuff and be back in just a few minutes, then."

"We'll be here," I assure her.

"Well, isn't she just a doll," Tori says once Ellie is gone. "I can see why you like her so much and enjoy her company."

"She is the sweetest. She's also not shy about telling both her dad and I she wants us to date. It was cute, all the not-so-subtle hints she was dropping when he was gone."

"That's a positive. If you've got the kid on your side, it will hopefully keep from any animosity building by her thinking you're trying to steal her dad away from her, or some crap like that."

"Yeah, I don't think that would happen. Not with how much he prioritizes their relationship. He worked so hard to make it to a team in California, only for it to almost not work out. Just as he was getting the news he'd made it on the roster, her mom was announcing she was moving for a promotion. They decided Ellie was old enough to make the choice where she wanted to live, and she chose to stay here so she didn't have to move schools or leave the one place she'd always called home."

"That is super sweet, and I love they let her make the final decision."

"I agree. While I know she misses her mom, she's been doing so good with all the changes," I tell Tori.

"That's good," she agrees.

"Okay, here's your choices of hoodies," I tell her, pulling out a couple, one being a Shockwaves hoodie Ryker brought over yesterday.

"Let me guess, this is the one you were going to wear today?" she asks, and I can't hide my excitement.

"Then, I won't be picking that one," she tells me, and picks another one I have from a trip to Utah a few years ago. "What does Ellie wear to his games?" she asks.

"Usually, a team T-shirt with a jersey on top," I tell her.

"Aww, how cute. Does she wear one with her dad's name and number on the back?"

"Of course. It's even signed. We were out in the commons once and someone asked how she got her jersey signed already. She didn't elaborate, just said her dad gave it to her. She was so sly about it. I don't think they even realized what she meant. It was great. We both walked away and had a good laugh over the exchange."

"Do you sit out in the main area?" Tori asks.

"No, they have a family and friends suite for everyone. They've been super nice to me, but I guess if things progress between Ryker and me, I won't just be attending as Ellie's handler."

"Dude, things are progressing, there's no if or when about it."

"Maybe," I agree as we hear another knock at the door and then it open and shut.

"I'm ready when you are," Ellie calls out.

We both grab our sweatshirts and head back out to the living room.

"Let me run Max out for a quick potty break and then we can head out," I tell both of them. "Anyone want to go with me?" I ask.

"I'm good," Tori says, sitting down on the couch. I don't miss how she hides her yawn. I can only imagine how much jet-leg she's feeling with the time difference and amount of travel she had to get back home.

"I'll stay up here, as well, that way I'm not distracting him from doing his business," Ellie tells me.

"Probably for the best," I tell her as I clip Max's leash to his collar. Even with a four-mile walk, he's eager to get back outside.

Once we're on the path, he starts his exploration with his nose to the ground as we walk down the way. It only takes a few minutes for him to lift his leg and pee for the first time. I know he usually has more in him, so I continue around the block. It doesn't fail, the next block he finds yet another place he needs to lift the leg and empty more of his bladder.

Just before we round the corner home, he stops me so he can empty the rest. I pull one of the dog poop bags from the carrying case, and scoop up what he left, tossing it in the ever-convenient trash can located just a few feet away.

"All right, Mr. Max has emptied his bladder and bowels, now's time for a special treat to hold him over until I return and can feed him dinner," I tell both Tori and Ellie. I put his treat in the kennel and he happily trots in, accepting it as he lies down while I lock the door so he's safe while I'm gone.

"Shall we?" I ask once I've finished everything.

"Yep." Ellie pops up from her place on the couch.

"Why are you in such a good mood?" I ask Ellie.

"Just excited to make it to another game," she tells me as we make our way down to my car.

I'm pretty good at remembering directions, so we forgo using the GPS on our way to the rink. We hit a little bit of heavy traffic as we take our exit for the stadium. It only takes a few minutes to get through it and to the player and family lot we have the pass for.

Ellie gave Tori a quick rundown of the game on our drive over, promising to point things out once she could actually visualize it in front of her on the ice.

"A private lot, how fancy," Tori muses as we pull in and park.

"There are a few more cars in here tonight, so I wonder if that means more people will be in attendance," I note.

"Maybe, or maybe some of the guys carpooled last time. They might not all have their cars yet, so that can make a difference." Ellie suggests.

"That makes sense." Tori states.

"But even if there are more people, we've got tickets for the box." Ellie tells Tori.

Our tickets are scanned, and we're given wristbands when we enter. Ellie leads the way to the entrance of the suite, where our tickets and wristbands are checked, once again, before we're let in.

"Holy crap, this place is swanky," Tori comments as she looks around. There are two tables with food and a small bar set up with a bartender pouring and mixing drinks.

"Welcome back," the bartender greets us as we walk his way.

"Nice to see you again," I tell him.

"Can I get any of you something to drink?"

"I'll take a Pepsi," Ellie tells him, and he hands over a freshly opened can.

"And for you ladies?" he asks, turning his attention back to Tori and me.

"I'm good with just a water, for now," I tell him.

"And for you, ma'am," he asks Tori.

"Can you do a whiskey sour?" she asks.

"Absolutely. Do you have a preference on the

whiskey?" he asks, grabbing a glass in preparation of making her drink.

"No, just make it however you'd normally make it, I'm not picky," she tells him, and he gets to work.

"Do you want to go over to the boards to watch warmups?" Ellie asks.

"Sure, lead the way," I tell her, and Tori and I follow as she leads us out of the suite and down a hall. We come to an opening that ends at the boards and plexiglass. A few other women and kids are milling around waiting for the guys to get out on the ice. It's only a few minutes before the PA announcer is calling out as the crowd cheers while the guys take the ice, led by the goalie, first. I watch in amazement as they file out, one at a time, all circling the ice, skating back and forth as they each seem to have their own rituals before they start to line up in groups and skate toward the goalie, who's ready to stop the pucks they send his way. Ryker notices us and slows down on his way by, giving us his trademark smile and wave. He fist-bumps the glass where Ellie has her fist pressed against it, and it is almost as cute as the toddler next to us with a jersey on that has daddy on the back with a player's number.

"Your son is just the cutest," I tell the woman holding him.

"Thank you," she says. "I don't think we've met, yet. I'm Sadie Wilkerson, Trevor Wilkerson is my husband, and this is our son Brady."

"It's nice to meet you, Sadie. I'm here with Ellie Jorgensen, she's Ryker's daughter."

"Welcome, are you her nanny?" she asks.

"No, just a friend. She's teaching me all about the game as I didn't know much before attending my first one on opening night with her."

"Oh, how fun. It's fast-paced, but you'll quickly catch on."

"I've enjoyed it so far. We've also watched a few of the away games together, and she can explain things a little easier at home when we aren't trying to talk over the arena noise."

"How fun," she says before turning her attention back to her son. A large man stops at the glass, he takes off one of his gloves and taps on the glass until he gets Brady's attention. The moment the boy sees his dad, his eyes light up and he'd crawl right through the glass if he could.

"Dada," he screeches in excitement.

"Daddy has to go play," Sadie tells him before they make a few more gestures through the glass at each other and then he's back out there with the team, skating as they switch up what they're doing on the ice.

"Damn, these guys are hot," Tori whispers so only I can hear.

"They are definitely easy on the eyes. I just couldn't tell you what ones are attached and what ones are single."

"I'll have to ask Ryker, later." She smirks. "Maybe if he gets to know me better, he'd be willing to introduce me to someone."

"You can try," I tell her, "But I make no promises."

Once the guys leave the ice, we make our way back to the suite. I grab a plate of food before taking my seat for the start of the game.

Tori and I have Ellie sit between us, this way she can explain things to both of us during the game. She's such a natural with explaining what's happening and why the refs blow the whistle each time.

The Shockwaves are off to a slow start, with the Stars striking first while on the power play. I've learned that means the other team did something bad and has to sit a player in the penalty box for a set amount of time, usually two minutes, unless they do something bad that warrants a harsher penalty.

"Why did the guy get to leave the box early?" Tori asks.

"If the team on the power play scores, then it voids the remaining time on the penalty because they scored. The only time it doesn't happen is if the penalty is a major, and then the team with the power play can score as many times as they want during the penalty without it ending early."

"Wow, that must suck if a team scores multiple times."

"Only if you're on the other team," Ellie chuckles.

"That's the truth," Tori agrees with her.

The Shockwaves finally score in the second period. Ryker skated up the side, making a quick pass to one of the other guys who did a cool little move, faking the goalie out before sending the puck flying into the back of the net. The crowd goes crazy as the goal horn blows loudly.

Unfortunately, the tied score doesn't last long, as the Stars score two more times before the end of the period. Our luck runs into the third period, where they add another goal to their tally before the final buzzer sounds.

I hate seeing the defeat on the faces of the players. I know they can't win every game, but it still sucks to see them like this.

CHAPTER 17

Ryker

I STAND under the hot spray of the water, the heat working its way into my exhausted muscles. Losing is never fun, but the level of defeat I'm feeling right now is like a hundred-pound weight across my shoulders. I knew, coming into a new team, the odds were not in our favor to win many games this season as we figure out how to work as a team. That's sometimes a hard pill to swallow for a team full of competitive guys. We take each and every loss personal.

"Hey, Cap," Jason Soaps calls out once I've stepped out of the shower with a towel wrapped around my waist.

"What's up, rookie?" I ask him. He's a good kid, just graduated college and was our first draft pick. He's a great player, and knows how to read the other team pretty damn well.

"Are you going out with everyone tonight?" he asks.

"I hadn't decided. Where are you guys headed?"

"Some sports bar not far away that Aiden found."

"I can probably stop by for a drink. Let me just check in with my daughter and make sure she's good and I'll let you know for sure," I tell him.

I make it back to my locker and quickly dry off. I get dressed in the suit I wore to the rink, but nix the tie. I add a little bit of gel to my hair, making it seem like I actually care what it looks like outside of my helmet. I need to find some time to go get it cut. I prefer to keep it on the shorter side, but time has gotten away from me and it's gotten long enough that I have to actually do something with it.

I pull my cell out, checking for any missed calls or texts. I see one from Ellie, and smile at the preview until I can open the full message.

> Sorry about the loss dad, you still kicked butt. And you'll always be my favorite player. {heart emoji}

> Thanks, Bean. Are you guys back home yet?

> Yeah, we just got back. Avery is out walking Max.

The guys wanted to go out, are you okay if I'm gone for an extra hour or two?

I'm fine dad, I was just going to look over my notes one last time for my test tomorrow and then get ready for bed, so if you're back after I'm in bed, I'll just see you tomorrow.

What time are you going to bed?

Probably around ten or so.

I'll be home before then

okay

Love you Ellie Bean.

Love you too, dad.

"Hey, rookie, is it just the guys coming or are your significant others joining at the bar?" I call out to Jason.

"Those that can are joining," he calls back.

Hey, what are you up to for the next hour or so?

AVERY

Tori and I were just going to BS until you got back, why what's up?

The guys all want to go out, do you ladies want to join us?

Maybe! Let me ask her once I'm back from my walk with Max. What about Ellie?

I love she cares so much about my daughter and her well-being.

I just was texting with her; she's looking over some notes for a test tomorrow and then headed to bed. I told her I'd be home well before she plans to go to sleep around ten.

Ah, yeah, she said she had some things to do when we got back but didn't elaborate as to what. I'm almost back, so I'll let you know shortly.

Sounds good, I've got to find out exactly where we're going, so take your time.

I slip my phone into my pocket and turn around to go find Aiden to figure out the plan for tonight.

"Where is everyone headed?" I ask Aiden once I find him coming out of the treatment room.

"It's called Southern Pacific Brewing and is over off of Treat Avenue."

"Sounds good. Avery and her friend might meet up with us, as well."

"Cool, yeah, whoever wants to come to drink the misery away with us is welcome to," he says as we make our way to his locker so he can get ready to leave.

I pull my phone out to let Avery know where we're going and see she already replied.

> Tori and I are in, just let me know when and where and we'll see you there.

> Southern Pacific Brewing, we should be headed that way in the next twenty or so minutes, so whenever you guys get there is fine.

> Looks like it's about a twenty-five-minute drive, so we'll leave in just a couple of minutes. Should I check in on Ellie before I leave?

Once again, her concern for my daughter doesn't go unnoticed. She's worming her way right into my heart, by way of her complete acceptance of Ellie.

> It's up to you, she was fine when I texted with her a few minutes ago.

> I'll just stop over and let her know we're headed out and make sure she's good.

> If it will make you feel better, then I'm not going to stop you. See you soon.

I gather my things, making sure I'm not leaving a huge mess in my locker for the equipment guys who are in charge of cleaning the locker room after every game. They are some of the unseen heroes of the sport. The way they can unpack and set up a locker room in record time; or the opposite, completely tear down a locker room and get things packed so we can make a flight out to the next city is nothing short of impressive.

"Does this bar know we're showing up?" I ask Aiden before I head out.

"Not exactly." He shrugs. "But I thought it was perfect as it's a pretty big place. I stopped in there yesterday for a burger and beer. I talked with the owner and manager, and they invited us all down whenever we wanted to drop in."

"All right, well, I'll head that way and see what kind of space I can secure for us," I tell him.

"I'll be right behind you." He tosses a few items in his bag before zipping it up and slinging it over his shoulder. We walk out together, all the way to the players' lot where a few family members mill around waiting on their player.

I toss my bag into the back seat before sliding behind the wheel. My car purrs to life, ever so quietly. I enter the address into my GPS and follow the line out of the parking lot.

"Are we opening one big tab, or individual ones?" the server asks after I secure a small section at the bar.

"You can do one," I tell him, and hand over my credit card. "Can you bring over four pitchers and a stack of glasses to start?" I ask.

"Sure can. Do you want them all the same or a variety?"

"A variety is perfect, and when you've got a second, I'll take a look at your menu."

"Of course, Cap, I'll be right back with that," he tells me before walking away.

I sit at a table in the corner, so far, going unnoticed by the other patrons in here tonight. I'm sure once my teammates start arriving, that won't last long, so I savor it while it does.

"Hey," a sweet voice greets, and I look up to find Avery and Tori standing across the table from me.

"Hey, yourself," I reply, getting up to come around the table to meet her properly. I pull Avery into me, needing her close tonight. "How was the drive over?"

"Fine. Not too bad of traffic since it's a Sunday night," she says.

"That's good," I tell her. A commotion catches my attention, so I look up and see a few of the guys entering. Sure enough, patrons take notice of them and follow as they make their way back to where I'm at with Avery and Tori. "And we've been spotted," I whisper into her ear.

"Did you think you'd be able to fly under the radar?" she asks, a little humor lacing her question.

"I was riding the wave as long as it lasted, but knew as soon as more guys arrived my luck was going to dwindle."

"I'm sure you'll be just fine." She pats my chest in fake sympathy.

"I can tell you what will make me feel all better," I whisper so only she can hear.

"What's that?"

"My name falling from your lips while I make you come again tonight," I answer.

"Oh," she says, her lips forming a perfect circle, and now all I can think of is them wrapped around my cock.

"Is that a yes for later?" I ask.

Avery nods her head, a large smile pulling at her lips.

"You just let me know when we're ready to get out of here and I'll happily make you mine tonight."

"Ellie's home," she reminds me. Our last two

nights together, we had a kid-free time as Ellie went to stay over at Steph's place.

"She's going to bed at ten, we can be at your place after that," I assure her.

"Okay," she easily agrees.

"Ryker!" Aiden bellows as he finally makes it over to where we're at.

"Aiden!" I copy his enthusiasm as he grips my outstretched hand and then pulls me into a man hug. "Let me introduce you. This is Avery," I say as I tug her closer into my side, staking my claim so all of these guys know she's mine and they need to back the fuck off if they had any ideas about her. "And this is her best friend, Victoria."

"You can call me Tori," she pipes up, offering up the nickname she prefers to go by.

"Nice to meet you," Aiden tells her, taking her hand and kissing her knuckles like he's prince fucking charming.

"Likewise," she tells him, and I don't miss the way they both look each other up and down. "Are you a hockey player, as well?" she asks.

"Yeah, I play on the same line as Ryker."

"Oh, cool. Today's game was my first one ever, so I'm still lost as to what was going on."

"Did you enjoy it?" I ask, curious how it went.

"I did. Ellie was incredibly helpful, trying to explain all the calls and what was happening."

"She's a pretty smart one," I confirm.

"I'm sure I could answer any of your burning questions about the game," Aiden tells her. We all start to file in, picking empty seats so we can fill the entire space in and hopefully keep unwanted people out.

"Let's do shots!" Tristan calls out as a server arrives with a drink tray covered in shot glasses. Someone must have ordered them as soon as they entered the bar, as there hasn't been a server over here since they've all filled in.

"Do you want one?" I ask Avery as I accept one of the glasses.

"No, I'm good. Plus, someone needs to stay sober to drive."

"Good point, but I also don't plan on getting drunk. One shot and probably one beer, plus, I'm ordering some food. I'm starving," I tell her.

"Then, I'll just be backup." She winks at me. I can't help it, the desire is too strong, so I pull her in for a kiss. "I missed you today," I say against her lips.

"We were only apart for a few hours," she reminds me.

"Sill too long," I tell her.

"Just wait until you leave again on a road trip. You're going to go through withdrawals," she teases.

"Don't remind me," I groan.

"Sorry for the wait. Here's the menu you asked to see," the server says, handing me the laminated sheet. I quickly scan it before he can leave the table.

"I'll take the bacon cheeseburger with fries and a side of ranch."

"I'll get everything put in right away. Can I get anyone else something?" he asks.

"Did you want anything?" I ask Avery and Tori.

"I'll just have a Coke," Avery tells him.

"Same for me," Tori adds.

"Perfect, I'll be right back."

"Are you sure you don't want something else?" I ask them both.

"We're sure," Avery insists, and I drop it. I'm not about to pressure either of them into something they don't want.

"Sorry about the outcome of the game," she says once we've settled onto one of the benches. Avery is tucked into my side, my arm around her as I attempt to hold her close.

"It happens. We can't win them all."

"You looked legitimately frustrated out on the ice."

"I was. I've never been the captain of a team, only ever an alternate, so the pressure of being the leader can be a little heavy, at times. I'm learning just like everyone else on this team what my place is. I'm confident I'll get there and figure everything out, I just need some time."

"I can't imagine any of it is easy. Maybe a little team bonding away from the ice will do you guys some good," she suggests, motioning around to everyone that has shown up here tonight. I'd say about two-thirds of the guys came, along with their wives or girlfriends, if they have one. The married guys with young kids, seem to be the ones not here, and I don't blame them. They want to spend every moment they can with their young families. We can bond while on road trips. If there's anyone who understands, it's me. That notion hits me, and I wonder if it's one of the reasons the management team wanted me to be the captain.

Our server returns with Avery's Coke, along with some other drinks ordered by people around our table.

"What's your week look like?" I ask Avery.

"Not much going on. I have a haircut, and this coming weekend is when I go to my parents' for dinner. Other than that, I don't have anything concrete planned. With Tori back, I'm sure I'll end up doing something with her. What about you?" she asks.

"Practice almost every day this week. We don't have an actual practice on game days, just an optional morning skate."

"How do days off work for you? I know some sports have, like, every Tuesday off, but that doesn't seem like a possibility for a hockey team."

"It isn't, and we don't have any mandatory days, usually. There are a couple days' break around the holidays, but usually not long enough for guys to fly home or anything like that, so a lot of years, one of the captains or coaches will host anyone who doesn't have a family to celebrate with."

"Will you be hosting guys this year?" she asks.

"I hadn't thought about it yet, to be honest with you. The holidays still feel so far away, even though I know they'll be here before we know it. I can't host too many with the size of my condo, but we'll figure it out in a few weeks."

We get pulled into a conversation with the entire table, and I feel myself start to relax and put aside the weight on my shoulders.

I check my watch and see it is already nine. I promised Ellie I'd be home before she went to bed, and I want to keep that.

"I need to head out. Do you want a ride home or did you drive here?" I ask Avery.

"Tori drove so she could go home from here, knowing you'd be able to give me a ride home."

"That was a good plan. Do you want to go say goodnight to her?" I ask. "I need to go settle up the tab, so I'll be a few minutes."

I head for the bar top while Avery moves to where Tori and Aiden are sitting and talking with one another. They're looking a little chummy, so I wonder if they're hitting it off tonight.

"Ready to get out of here?" I ask Avery once I'm back at the table.

"Yep," she says, popping the p.

I slip my hand into hers, linking our fingers together as we walk out of the bar and to my car.

"Do you need me to drive?" she asks as we reach her car.

"I'm good. I drank two glasses of water after my one beer and shot, plus, I've had the burger and fries, but thanks for the offer," I state as I open Avery's door for her. I wait until she's in, then close it before I jog around the front of the car to the driver's side. I slide in and get situated before I program the GPS with the address of the condo. I still don't know my way around very well, but that is why GPS was created.

"I was thinking some, today," I tell Avery as I break the silence.

"What's that?" she asks, looking my way.

"Ellie liked the setup we had while I was gone, and she's been begging me to keep with it, so it brings me to this conversation. Are you sure you're good with looking after her while I'm gone?"

"Of course, I am!" she insists.

"Then, it's settled, you'll stay with her on most trips. Maybe I can fly the two of you to a city or two throughout the season."

"That sounds like fun," she tells me.

Sunday night traffic is nothing like other days. Most people are apparently home and getting ready for bed. We're able to make it with no real delays. One red light, otherwise, they were all green for us.

"I'm going to go spend a little time with Ellie. Will you be staying up past ten?" I ask.

"I don't see why I won't be, I'm still pretty wired."

"Then, I'll come over once she's off to bed."

"Sounds like a plan," she says as we head upstairs.

Before we part at her door, I push her up against the wall, wanting just a taste of what's to come later. Our lips connect and, once again, I feel centered. Like everything in my world is perfect. When this woman is in my orbit, my entire life feels like it is balanced and going as it should.

Avery pushes me back a step, one hand on my chest, the other going to her kiss-swollen lips. "If you don't go spend time with your daughter, you're going to miss your chance."

"You're right," I agree, and quickly check the time. It is nine thirty-five, so I need to hustle. "I'll see you in a half-hour or so. "

"Take your time. I'm going to take Max out for a bit."

"Please be careful."

"I'm always careful. It also helps that Max is pretty possessive of me. He'd defend me against anyone that tried to do anything to me."

"I sure hope so. See you soon." I lean in and give her one more quick kiss before I'm pulling away and walking to my door.

I find Ellie on the couch, her notebook spread open on her lap, but she's sound asleep.

"Ellie Bean," I whisper her name. I try shaking her shoulder to wake her up without startling her.

"Hey, Dad," she greets, giving me a sleepy smile.

"Why don't you head to bed, kiddo?" I suggest. She's obviously exhausted, so there isn't any reason why she needs to force herself to stay awake.

"I must have passed out while studying," she muses, looking around at the papers strewn about. She starts to collect them, organizing exactly how she wants them for her binder. I just stay back, letting her do it all. "How was the bar?" she asks once all her papers are picked up and ready to take back to school tomorrow.

"It was fun. We all had a good time. Everyone else that showed up was still going strong when we called it a night."

"Why'd you leave, then?" she questions.

"I made a promise to you, and I wanted to make sure I had time with you tonight."

"Thanks, Dad. Sorry I fell asleep on the couch already. I'm going to have to head to bed sooner than later. I've got a big test tomorrow and I need to be well-rested."

"Of course," I tell her as I relax back on the couch, kicking my feet up on the coffee table.

"See you in the morning, Dad. I love you."

"Love you, too, kiddo. I'm going next door for a

little bit, if you need me," I tell her so she'll know where I am, if needed. All I get in response is a raised hand.

My own exhaustion kicks up a notch as I sit here, relaxing back. I give Ellie a few more minutes to fall asleep before I head next door. I quickly change out of my suit and into a pair of athletic shorts and a T-shirt.

"I almost thought you'd given up on me," Avery says when she opens her door and lets me in. Max is asleep on his bed in the living room. He must be exhausted if he isn't up investigating who's coming into his home.

"Never. I was just talking to Ellie and then dodging falling asleep, myself, on the couch for the night."

"Is she ready for her test tomorrow?" Avery asks.

"As far as I know. She's never asked me to quiz her or anything, but I know my daughter, and getting good grades is a priority."

I join Avery on the couch. She directs me to lie down, then she mirrors my position so we're facing one another on our sides. "There, now we can talk while comfortable."

"Or I can kiss you easier." I smirk and bring her in for a kiss. It doesn't take long for both of us to deepen it. We can, and do, make out like two horny teenagers. Our hands roam one another's bodies as we continue to learn each other's wants. "Is it bad

I'm content just making out with you?" I ask when we separate for a breath.

"Not at all. I like kissing you," Avery says. "I also like just being in your arms. They're warm and strong. I feel protected and cherished when right here." She shimmies her body, trying to get closer, yet not accomplishing anything.

"You fit perfectly in my arms, almost like we were both created for one another."

"Something like that," she says. Something must be on her mind with the way she nibbles on her bottom lip and worry lines pop between her furrowed brows.

"What's on your mind?" I ask as I smooth a thumb over her brows.

"What are we doing? What is this thing between us to you?" she whispers.

"I'd like to think we're exploring this connection, this kinetic pull we seem to have toward one another. I've never been one for labels, but this feels different, feels right."

"Does it mean we're dating? Friends with benefits?" she questions.

"I can be a jealous man, so friends with benefits doesn't work for me. I want you all to myself. I want you to be mine, so as cheesy and high schoolish as it sounds, Avery, would you like to be my girlfriend?"

"I'd love nothing more," she agrees before pressing her lips to mine. We quickly become a tangled mess of limbs as we attempt to tug articles of clothes off.

"It truly should be illegal how sexy your muscles are," Avery muses once my shirt is off and she can easily ogle my body.

"I could say the same about your tits," I say as I get a handful of them, paying special attention to her sensitive nipples.

"Are you a breast man?" she asks, and works at shoving my shorts down. My cock springs free between the two of us. My eyes about roll into the back of my head when she wraps her hand around my shaft and starts stroking me.

"Sorry, what was the question?" I stammer out.

"Are you a breast man?" she asks, just as her hand shuttles over the crown of my cock.

"Yes, very much so, along with whatever in the hell you're doing to me right now."

"I thought so." She smirks, and I kiss it right off her face. I slip my hand into her leggings, finding her with no panties. My fingers slide through her wet folds until I'm sinking two fingers deep into her channel. My thumb works her clit as I pump in and out, mimicking her strokes of my cock.

CHAPTER 18

Avery

"YES, YES, YES," I chant. My orgasm is just about to explode as Ryker fucks me with his fingers. His teeth graze my neck, my pulse pounding against his lips as he nips and sucks at my exposed skin.

"Give it to me, Avery. Come on my fingers. I can't wait to lick them clean, get your sweet taste on my tongue," he coaches. My fist is wrapped around his shaft, working up and down his length at a rapid speed. His pre-cum acts as the best lubricant.

"I'm," I start to tell him as my orgasm wracks my body. I go completely rigid before resting against Ryker's body. Thankfully, he's positioned in a way he can support my weight, especially when I'm bone-less, thanks to my orgasm.

"Delicious," Ryker whispers into my ear. I shift my head so I can look at him, and he's sucking the fingers that were just buried deep inside of me. I didn't actually think he'd do it, but holy hell does it turn me on.

I sit up, then stand from the couch. I motion for Ryker to lie down flat, and he does so immediately. I climb back on, straddling his hips in the process. I shuttle over his shaft with my wet center.

"Do you have a condom in your wallet?" I ask, hoping he does.

"No, I didn't bring it over with me, but we can have fun in other ways." He winks at me.

"Or we could go without…" I trail off. "I'm clean and on birth control. No pressure if you'd rather not, I'd understand."

He cups my face and pulls me to him. "Are you sure? I'm clean as a whistle and have never gone without. I'm completely fine with waiting, if you'd rather have one."

I kiss him briefly, pushing up on my knees until I have enough space to grip his hard shaft. I line it up with my entrance and sink down. The velvety feel of his bare skin against my own is like nothing I've ever experienced.

"Holy fucking shit, Aves," he hisses. It's the first time he's ever shortened my name, and I love it. "You feel so damn good riding my cock bare."

"So good," I agree as my orgasm builds.

Ryker pinches my nipples, the pinch of pain

sending a bolt of electricity straight to my core. He slides one of his hands down my torso until his fingertips find purchase on my clit. He alternates circling it, followed by pinching, and finally pressing hard down on the bundle of nerves until I explode on his cock. My body arches back as euphoria takes over.

"So tight and wet for me," Ryker pants into my ear as he takes over, pounding into me as he finds his own release. "Yes, baby," he whispers as we both relax, enjoying the feel of each other's bodies after our mutual releases.

"We should probably get cleaned up," I finally say after we've lain on the couch for a good ten to fifteen minutes. If I'm not careful, I could easily just drift off to sleep in Ryker's arms. He's so warm and my body fits so nicely tucked against his.

"Probably," he chuckles in agreement.

I go to push off of him, but he cups my cheeks as I do and pulls me in for a slow and languid kiss. The way he devours me is like nothing I've ever experienced in the past. It makes me feel powerful in a way I never have before.

"Did you want to come shower with me?" I ask, deciding in this moment I'm not going to shy away from what I want with this man.

"Lead the way, beautiful," he says. I stand and offer him my hand. I lead us to my bathroom, dropping his hand so I can turn the shower on and then pull out two clean towels. I set them on the countertop, then strip my clothes all the way off. We never managed to stop long enough to completely undress out on the couch.

I step into the shower, the warm spray hitting my skin and providing a much-needed jolt of heat. Ryker steps in and stands in front of me, his sinewy body on display to me. It's so not fair just how defined his muscles are. "I don't know what I did in this life to get so lucky, but I'd do it all over again if it means I got to stand here in this shower and look at you naked," he tells me, his eyes hooded with his desire for me.

"I could say the same about you," I tell him as I trail a hand from his pecs to the happy trail. His cock springs up the closer I get to it. "It looks like someone is ready to play again." I smirk and wrap my fist around his glorious cock.

"Only when I'm around you," he says, pulling me until our bodies are flush. He kisses me deeply, my body instantly ready for whatever pleasure I want to throw at it.

We make out, but that's as far as we go. Ryker reaches for my shampoo and adds a small amount to his palm. "Turn around and I'll wash your hair," he offers, and I do as instructed. He's so gentle with the way he massages the soap into my scalp. Taking his time as he does a thorough job.

"If you keep spoiling me with this kind of treatment, I might need you in every shower I take."

"That can be arranged." He smirks, dropping a kiss to my cheek. He tips my head back and helps guide the water as the soap rinses out.

"I know we decided what this is between the two of us, but how does it translate when we're not in the confines of these four walls, specifically, when we're around Ellie?" I ask once we're out of the shower and drying off.

"You know she's going to be ecstatic, so don't feel like we need to hide from her. As far as PDA goes, I'm comfortable with some around her. We don't need to embarrass anyone. I can contain my need to always be touching you, but only around my daughter." He smirks as he reaches out and tugs the top of my towel, causing it to fall to the floor.

"Ryker," I try and scold, but I can't stop my smile and laugh.

"Avery," he replies, his own amusement evident in his voice.

"You're incorrigible." I laugh and attempt to push him away. It does nothing but make him tighten his hold on me, his fingers digging deeper into my sides as I squirm against him.

"Only for you," he states. I look up and can't get over the way he's looking down at me. I've only ever read about it in romance novels, but to experience it firsthand is completely different.

"Hey, Dad," Ellie calls out as she walks through the door. Ryker and I are lying down on the couch watching a movie. "Oh my god, *yes!*" Ellie calls out when she sees the two of us curled up together. "Does this mean the two of you are dating?" she asks.

"Yep," I confirm, giving her a big smile as Ryker hugs me tighter.

"About time." She smiles big. "Does this mean I can stay with you when Dad's out of town all the time?"

"I'm perfectly fine with you staying with me," I tell her.

"If that's what the two of you want, then I'm okay with it," Ryker chimes in.

"Thank you, Dad!" Ellie says, spinning in a circle due to her excitement.

"You're welcome, Ellie Bean. How was Steph's?"

"Good. We just hung out, for the most part. Went to the mall last night for an hour or so."

"Did you get anything fun?" I ask.

"No, her mom was looking for something. We mainly went to hit up the food court."

"Do you have any homework you need to get done?" Ryker asks her.

"Nope. I planned on studying a little later for a

quiz we have this week, but it's nothing major and I already know the material."

"That's my girl," Ryker praises her.

"I do need to go to Target, though," she says.

"For what?" he asks.

Her eyes slide between the two of us, almost nervous like. "I need some girly things," she finally says, and I catch on right away.

"More makeup crap?" Ryker asks, and I can hear the disdain in his voice.

I elbow him in the ribs. "Don't be a jerk, there's nothing wrong with makeup or any other girly products," I tell him, standing up for Ellie.

"Not makeup, Dad, feminine products. Like, pads and tampons."

"That's enough, say no more. Here's my credit card," he tells her, grabbing his wallet and handing over his card.

I can't help the belly laugh as it bursts from my lips. "Are you seriously squeamish about periods, pads, and tampons?" I ask, sitting up so I can get a good look at him.

"When it comes to my daughter, yes," he states, looking a little green.

"Oh, my god." I laugh at his uncomfortable state. "This is priceless. You'll stick a tampon up your nose during a hockey game to stop a nosebleed, but your daughter asks to go buy some for their intended purpose and they, all of a sudden, become an item you pretend doesn't exist."

"I get it." He laughs. "It is a completely normal bodily function. I'm just not used to dealing with it from my daughter. I still look at her as a little five-year-old, not the fifteen-year-old she is now."

"Your little girl is growing up," I say as I pat his cheek. "I'll take you to Target," I tell Ellie as I look up at her.

"Yes!" She cheers. "Can we get Starbucks and look around?" she asks.

"Of course. We've got your dad's credit card, after all." I smirk and look back at Ryker.

"Take it, buy whatever it is your little hearts desire. I'll stay here and find something manly to do," he states.

"You could join us, if you'd like," I offer.

"No, you go have a girls' trip to Target. I could get some dinner started while you're gone and we could all eat together," he suggests.

"That works for me. How about you, Ellie?"

"Fine by me," she agrees.

"Do you need anything from the store?" I ask him. If I'm going with his credit card, I might as well offer to pick up anything that he might need.

"I've got a short list started in the kitchen, do you mind taking it and picking the items up?"

"Not at all," I tell him before he pulls me in for a quick kiss.

"Thank you for saving me," he says against my lips.

"Anytime. You can pay me back later." I wink at him before standing up and gathering the list and my things before Ellie and I head out the door.

CHAPTER 19

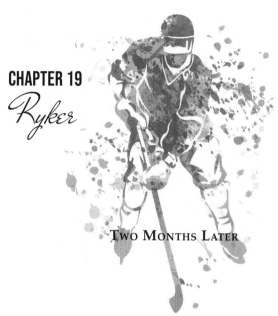

Ryker

Two Months Later

I'M STRETCHED out on my side on the couch, Avery's body pressed against my own as we watch an episode of the Bachelor. I grumbled when Ellie flipped to the channel, but gave in, knowing that these two love this show. I don't really care, I just bury my face in the crook of Avery's neck and enjoy the time I have with them tonight.

"I can't believe he sent her home!" Ellie gasps. "After he told her he loved her, what a jerk!"

"She was definitely caught off guard," Avery agrees with her.

"She's better off without him, he's such a jerk. I

hope that the last girls tell him no and turn and walk away," Ellie says.

"You know not many of these couples stay together after the show is done taping, right?" I add to the conversation.

"Yeah, I think at this point, most people just go on this show for the fame. Hoping to grow a following so they can become the next big social media influencer or write a tell-all book." Avery replies.

"Please promise me you'll never audition for this kind of reality TV," I sit up slightly and say to Ellie.

"Never. I don't like being the center of attention, so no way am I getting in front of a camera for trashy, scripted TV."

"That's my girl," I praise. "Oh, I have something to run by the two of you."

"What's that?" Avery asks.

"Some teams plan a mom or dad's trip, where they take all the available players' moms or dads on a road trip. However, this season, the front office wants to make it a family trip. Is that something the two of you would be interested in attending? It is a long weekend trip, so you'd only miss school for one day, Ellie."

"Sounds fun. If you want to go, Ellie, I'm game," Avery tells her.

"As long as it isn't during mid-term week, I'd love to go," Ellie confirms.

"It's in two weeks, is that mid-terms?" I ask.

"Nope, so we should be good to go!" Ellie confirms.

"Awesome, I'll let the front office know to expect the two of you."

"HOW WAS YOUR FLIGHT?" I ask Avery as I pull her in for a kiss.

"Pretty fancy. I've never flown private before."

"Did you get all checked in to your room?"

"Yes, they had the key card packets ready for us when we arrived. Didn't even have to stop at the front desk."

"That's how it is when we arrive," I tell her.

"How was your flight?" she asks, smoothing down the lapels of my suit jacket.

"Fine. Pretty typical flight," I tell her. The team arrived earlier today as we came in from St. Louis. The families are only joining the team for the game against Chicago tomorrow night. "What was Ellie up to?" I ask, pulling Avery a little tighter against me. The way she's tucked into my body has my cock swelling in my slacks, and the desire to take her inside my room and ravish her is strong.

"She was going to take an hour and finish up a paper she needs to email to her teacher. She was working on it most of the flight."

"So, I have you to myself for a little while?" I ask before bringing my lips to her neck. I suck lightly just behind her ear, where I know it drives her crazy.

"Yes," she whispers. "What did you have in mind?"

"Come with me." I step back and grab her hand, pulling her to the elevator so we can go up to my room.

I slam the door behind me and immediately press Avery up against the wall. My lips claim hers as I press my aching cock into her belly.

"Fuck, I need to be inside you," I groan against her lips.

She arches her back and presses her hips forward. I reach down and grip the back of her thigh, lifting her leg up and around my hip. "I need you," she moans.

That's all I need to pull away and drop to my knees. I quickly unbutton and draw the zipper of her jeans down, then tug them over her hips. I snag the waistband of her panties and take them with, all the way down until she's stepping out of them.

I draw my nose up the inside of her leg until my tongue finds her wet center. I trace around her clit and can already feel it starting to pulse with her need.

"Fuck, baby, you're so ready for me," I praise, and slip two fingers inside her wet center.

"Ryker," she cries out as her fingers find purchase

in my hair. Scraping and tugging at my hair just spurs me on to send her over the cliff.

"Come for me, Avery," I pull back and instruct her. I blow on her clit before biting down on it. I soothe it with an immediate lap of my tongue just as she detonates. Her body sags against the wall and me, causing me to have to pull back so I can support her.

I get to my feet, Avery leaning on me the entire time, so I scoop her up and carry her to the bed. I set her on the edge, then reach down and pull her T-shirt off over her head, followed by her bra.

I love her perky tits. The way they fit into my hands, the way her nipples tighten into little buds when I lick and suck at them has my dick twitching just thinking about it.

"You're a little overdressed," she says, flicking her eyes to mine.

"Not for long," I tell her as I toss my suit jacket on the chair in the corner of the room. My slacks and dress shirt are quick to follow. I step between her legs, gripping my cock through my boxer briefs.

"You're still overdressed." She smirks, her hands coming up to trail down my abs. She tucks a fingertip into the waistband on each of my hips and slowly pulls my boxer briefs down. My cock springs free, bouncing against my abs before pointing directly at her. "Mhmm," Avery hums as she grips my cock and leans forward, taking me into her mouth.

"Babe," I grit out, the warmth of her mouth as it engulfs my length has me ready to blow my load before we even get started. Her fist trails her lips as she bobs back and forth along my length. The moment her tongue slides around my crown, I pull from her magical grasp and push her up the mattress. I've had enough foreplay. I need to be balls deep inside this woman, now.

"I wasn't done," she pouts.

"Either am I," I tell her as I capture her swollen lips. I slide a finger between her folds, making sure she's still good and wet for me before I line my cock up with her entrance and push inside. The immediate feeling of being home rushes over me. I slowly pull out, pushing back inside. I take my time building the speed of my thrusts, driving us both crazy in the process.

"Ryker, harder," Avery cries.

I roll my hips, allowing me to hit her g-spot in a new way. She cries out in pleasure, so I do it again and again.

"I need you there," I tell her, holding back my release until she's ready for her own.

"Yesyesyes," she chants in my ear. I swivel my hips one more time, slamming into her with every ounce of control I have. She explodes on my cock, taking me right over the edge with her.

I collapse forward, my head resting on her chest, between her breasts. I watch as she heaves for a breath, all while I do the same. As her breathing slows, I look up and see the most beautiful glow on her skin.

"Welcome to Chicago," I tell her before kissing her lightly on the lips.

"If this is the kind of welcome I get on road trips, sign me up for more," she jokes.

"I could arrange for that," I tell her.

"Someone has to stay home and take care of Ellie," she reminds me.

"I know, but I do like the sound of you coming out on the road a time or two, even if it is just for a weekend game."

"We'll see," she says before pushing me back so she can head to the bathroom.

"WHAT ARE WE DOING TOMORROW?" Ellie asks once we've all finished dinner. With all the family members here with us tonight, the team had dinner catered for us in one of the hotel's banquet rooms.

"We have a free morning and then we've got a walking tour downtown while the guys all take their afternoon naps," Avery tells her.

"Are we going to the arena with the team in the afternoon?" Ellie asks.

"No, they'll take us there about an hour before the

game starts. We're sitting up in a box, and dinner will be served in there."

"Sounds good. Maybe we can do a little shopping while we're on our tour," she says.

"Or we can head out in the morning, if you'd like. Breakfast will be in here, tomorrow, but it is just a come as you want leisurely kind of thing."

"What is it that you want to go shopping for?" I ask.

"Nothing in particular. Just window shopping, for the most part, maybe pick up a souvenir or two," she says.

"Did you bring your credit card?" I ask Avery.

"It's in my wallet," she says, smiling at me.

"Good. Make sure you use it if you girls go shopping."

"We'll see," she smirks, knowing that it drives me crazy when she won't let me pay for things.

"Ellie, make sure she uses my card if either of you buys anything this weekend."

"I'll see what I can do, Dad," she replies.

We mingle with my teammates and their families. Most of the single guys just have their parents along, or a sibling. The married or attached guys have wives, girlfriends, and a few other kids here this weekend, as well.

"I'm ready for bed," Avery says while yawning into her hand.

"Then, let's get you off to bed," I suggest. We say

goodnight to everyone who is still hanging out, just shooting the shit. I walk Ellie and Avery to their room, waiting to enter while Ellie pulls her card out and pushes the door open.

"Are you coming in for a little bit?" Avery asks.

"Sure, but not for long, I need to get to bed, myself."

"I'm going to take a quick shower before getting into bed," Ellie says. She stops in front of me and I pull her in for a hug.

"Love you, kiddo," I tell her as I kiss the top of her head.

"Love you, too, Dad."

"Have fun tomorrow."

"I will. Score a goal for me?" she asks, and I can't help but smile. She's asked me that question before so many of my games, I've lost count.

"I'll see what I can do," I tell her.

Appeased with my answer, she gathers her things and heads into the bathroom.

"Did you have a good time tonight?" I ask Avery as I gather her into my arms.

"The best," she says and nuzzles into my chest.

"Thank you for coming this weekend."

"Thank you for inviting me. I wouldn't have missed it for anything."

"Let it be known that you have an open invitation to any of my games, home or away. I want you at them any chance I can have you there. Knowing that you're there cheering me on, wearing my number on your back, does shit to me, in here," I tell her, tapping my hand against my chest, "and in here," I say, moving my hand to tap against my temple. "I know it's been fast between the two of us, but I love you, Avery, and I can't go another day without telling you just that."

Tears fill her eyes and I internally cuss myself out for dropping the love bomb on her.

"Well, it's a good thing you do, because I love you, too, Ryker. I think I've loved you since the moment Max tried to lick you to death in the hallway. You are an incredible man, father, and boyfriend. I feel like I'm just as lucky as you are in this relationship."

"I assure you, I'm the lucky one. I don't know what I did in this life to deserve a woman like you, but I'm sure glad I did it because I don't plan on ever letting you go."

CHAPTER 20

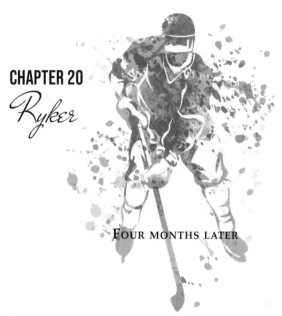

Ryker

Four months later

The final buzzer sounds, our inaugural season coming to an end. New teams are never projected to do very well in their first season, for sure. We did okay, but not good enough to make the playoffs. While every player's goal is to make it to the end, being handed the greatest cup in sports, the likelihood of being on that team is one in thirty-two. Odds aren't in your favor. Even knowing that, the loss still stings. The elimination after we poured our blood, sweat, and tears onto the ice these last six or so months doesn't make it any less disappointing.

We make it to the locker room, the guys mostly quiet at the realization tomorrow is the day we clean out our lockers. Some of the players filling the room today won't be back when camp rolls around in the fall. They'll be traded or signed with new teams, or possibly even retire before then. I look around and see all the good that came out of this first year. The bonds we made, the celebrations we had after milestone games.

"Can I have your attention?" I call out into the room. Since it was already quiet, all eyes turn my way quickly. "I know this loss is bittersweet, but I want each and every one of you to know how proud I am of the effort we put forth night after night. It isn't easy being the pieced-together group of players a new team has to work with, but we came out and showed the naysayers we do have what it takes, and with some time and hard work, we'll get there. We won more games than expected, or we were projected to win this year, and that alone is a huge accomplishment. I've been honored to play with all of you this past season, not only as a teammate, but as your captain. I didn't take the title lightly and I hope I did everyone proudly."

"Cap, cap, cap," the rumbles start to build as the guy's chant.

"All right," I yell out, holding up a hand to hopefully calm the locker room down. "Let's get showered and changed. We've got a lot of people waiting on us to celebrate our accomplishments," I remind them.

I walk into the private reception room at a local hotel. The place is decked out in black and red everything. Streamers, balloons, flowers. Even the tablecloths, plates, and napkins are in the team's colors.

"Hey, baby," I greet Avery. I pull her into my arms as my lips find hers in a searing kiss. "You ladies outdid yourselves," I tell her as I take another look around the room.

"Only the best for you and the guys. Plus, we had fun planning all of this," she assures me.

We were eliminated from making the playoffs weeks ago, so we knew tonight was our final game of the season, which gave the ladies plenty of time to plan the party.

My teammates all start filing in, along with their families or dates. I've enjoyed getting to know this group of guys, especially Jason, Aiden, Tristan, Damien, and Blake. We've grown closer as a group, and I can only believe it will continue over the next few seasons. We all have multi-year contracts, which should help with the chemistry that is needed to make a good team. Toward the end of the season, we'd finally started to find our chemistry with each other, but unfortunately, it was just too late to make a difference in making it to the playoffs this year.

"Hey, Tori," I greet Avery's best friend. "Thanks for helping Avery with all of this." I motion to the room.

"Of course. You know I love a good party and will take any excuse to hang out with our girl."

"You and me both," I chuckle as Aiden approaches my side. I don't miss the way Tori looks him up and down, nor the way he does the same to her. "You two know each other?" I ask.

"We met after I went to my first game and then met up with you guys at the bar, afterward," Tori tells me.

"Ah, that's right," I remember back to the night. I also remember Avery mentioning the two of them looked a little cozy in the corner together.

"Well, have fun. I'm going to go talk to Jason for a minute." I leave them to eye fuck each other. Maybe they'll go home together and get it over with to get it out of their systems.

"Captain," Jason greets, slapping me on the back as I stop next to him. He's circled around with Damien and Blake, one of our defensemen and our starting goalie. "How's it going?" he asks.

"Can't complain. I've got a beer in my hand," I say, holding it up, "no practice for a couple of months, just some relaxing in my future. How about you?"

"Olivia's been busy planning the wedding, so I'm sure I'll be roped into helping with it now that the season is over."

"That's right. When is the big day?" I ask.

"August first, so mark your calendar. Invitations should be going out this week, I believe."

"Will do. Are you getting married back in Indianapolis?" I ask.

"No, we're doing a destination wedding in Hawaii. She's from a pretty small town in Iowa and didn't think it could handle the number of guests we'd need to invite. I didn't care where it was. My mom actually suggested Hawaii and Olivia loved the idea. She flew out over her spring break with our moms, and they got everything set up with the venue."

"Happy for you, man, she seems like a great girl," I tell him.

"The best, I'm definitely the lucky one in our relationship."

"That's usually the way it goes, but when you find a good one, you don't let them go," I agree just as I catch Avery's eye from across the room. She flashes me a smile, one that's just for me, and promises of more to come later. With all the wedding talk with Jason, it gives me visions of Avery in a white dress, walking down an aisle to me. We haven't even been together a year yet, but I don't need more time to know she's my forever. With the idea stuck in my head, I'm suddenly itching to run to the nearest jewelry store to buy a ring.

The party presses into the early morning hours, most of the guys are well past drunk, at this point.

Thankfully, the ladies thought ahead and planned for transportation to safely get everyone home. "You ready to get out of here?" I ask Avery.

"So ready," she says as a yawn slips out. "My feet are killing me and I'm ready to close my eyes and sleep for a day."

"You should have told me earlier you were ready to go."

"I'm fine, the exhaustion just kicked in a few minutes ago. Sitting down was my downfall." She chuckles and lays her head on my shoulder.

"We're out," I call out to the small group of guys still here. "See you guys for locker checkout in the afternoon. One o'clock sharp, don't be late," I remind them.

"Aye, aye, Captain," Aiden calls out. He loves busting my balls and saying that whenever he can slip it in.

"Night, fuckers." I laugh as I follow Avery out the door.

We slip into the back of a town car; the driver already has the address. I tug Avery so she's right next to me. "Thank you for everything," I tell her again. I slide my lips along the exposed column of her neck, kissing and sucking on the sensitive skin.

"My pleasure," she replies, a little breathlessly.

"I'll absolutely pleasure you." I smirk against her skin.

"Smartass," she laughs before gasping when I latch on to her skin, nipping at it as my desire amps up. I've got a very nice buzz going and am ready to get this woman home, naked and underneath me. "You need to control yourself until we're home," she whispers to me.

I don't need to put on a show for the driver, so I pull back and give her a quick chaste kiss. "There'll be more of that when we get home," I promise.

"I wouldn't expect anything less," she says, and runs her fingers through my hair.

"Jason was telling me a little about his and Olivia's wedding. Said to expect an invitation soon, as it is in August and in Hawaii. Maybe we can make a family vacation out of it?" I suggest.

"I could definitely get on board with that. Will Ellie be back from Texas by then?"

"Even if she isn't, I can fly her out, if she wants to go, otherwise, we can make a romantic getaway for just the two of us." I smirk, and the thought of Avery in nothing but string bikinis for a week is something I could be on board with.

"What's so funny?" she asks, rolling her eyes at me like she already knows what's floating through my mind.

"If it's just the two of us, you can spend the entire time in a bikini."

"I knew you were going to say something like that." She shakes her head at me. "I'm a little shocked you didn't just go straight to being naked the entire time."

"Being naked would mean other people might see you, and I'm not okay with people seeing what's mine," I growl in her ear. "You're mine and only mine."

"Hmm, I love it when possessive caveman Ryker comes out."

"I'll show you caveman in a few minutes," I promise just as the car comes to a stop outside the building. The driver gets out and opens the door. I step out and offer Avery a hand to take while she exits. "Thank you," I tell the driver, handing him a tip.

"Thank you, sir. Have a good night." He tips his head to us before rounding the car and getting back into the driver's seat. I escort Avery inside the building and up the elevator.

"Can we go straight to my place, or do you need to let Max out?" I ask.

"I took him to doggie daycare and let him play, and then just stay the night since I knew I'd be gone all day between the game and party."

"Probably a good idea."

"It was either that or get a dog walker to come in a few times, but even with a walker I didn't want him either in the kennel all the time or left out where he could get into trouble. He loves going to play with all the other dogs and I don't have to worry about his safety."

"Works for me. Now, I can ravish you without worrying about if he needs to go out to pee or not."

"Exactly," she agrees as I lead her inside my condo.

With Ellie gone for the night, the condo is empty. As soon as the door closes behind us, I flip the lock and turn my sights on Avery.

I grab her hand, pulling her gently into my arms. "I love you," I tell her. It isn't the first time we've said those three words to one another, far from it, but I like to remind her.

"I love you, too." She kisses me lightly.

"I know I say thanks a lot, but I genuinely do mean it. You stepped in and supported me when I needed it the most this season. I couldn't have made it through the season without your support with Ellie, or without your guidance in handling my stress. You've become one of the most important people in my life and I just need you to know that."

"There isn't anywhere else I'd rather be. You've become one of my best friends, Ryker, and I don't know what I'd do without Ellie and you in my life."

I cup Avery's cheeks. "Fuck it, I definitely didn't plan on doing this right here, right now. I haven't even gone to the damn store yet," I mumble under my breath, but know Avery hears every word the way her eyes light up. "Avery Reid, you are the love of my life, a woman my daughter not only adores but looks up to and respects. Besides Ellie, I'd like for you to be the most important woman in my life. Please say you'll marry me and complete this family we've created together."

"Yes." She nods her head yes as her tears fall. I wipe them away with my thumbs before I bring my lips to hers.

"Thank fuck," I mumble. "We can go pick you out a ring this week, get you whatever you want."

"I can't believe you just proposed and we're getting married. Ellie is going to be so excited when we tell her," Avery says. "She asked me a few weeks ago if I thought we'd get married."

"And what did you tell her?" I ask, curious what she thought, then.

"I said I was confident our relationship was headed in that direction, but it wasn't something I could put a time limit on."

"How quickly can I convince you to marry me?" I ask.

Avery gives me a puzzled look as she ponders the question. "Well, I don't know. I'm not usually one that wants to be the center of attention, but I am a girl, after all. I've dreamed of what my wedding day will be like since I can remember."

"And I want you to have it all. I just want to know how long it will take to pull together."

"No idea. Let me have a few days to wrap my

head around the fact we're getting married. Then, we can sit down with a calendar and figure out what works with your schedule."

"I can agree to those terms. I'll make it known, I'd prefer if it happens this year, but also realize weddings take time to plan, so if it can't happen until next year, I'll understand."

"I'll make it worth your while, no matter when it is." She smirks and lifts up on her toes to kiss me.

I drop my hands to her ass, hauling her up until her legs are wrapped around my waist. "Now that we've got everything settled, I need to be inside of you, fiancée," I tell her as I take her to bed.

CHAPTER 21
Avery

"Ryker," I moan. His face between my legs is quite the way to wake up. He laps at my clit, my body quickly ready to react to his pleasure.

"Morning, baby," he says once I've regained composure after coming on his tongue. "Or should I say, fiancée?" he corrects himself.

"Fiancée." I roll the word around, loving the sound of the title. I still can't believe he proposed last night.

"I'll be a few hours at the rink this afternoon, but afterward, I can pick you up and we can go look at rings, if you want."

"Okay," I giddily agree. "When are we going to tell Ellie?"

"Whenever she gets home, or when do you want to tell her?" he asks.

"When she gets home is fine with me. I don't think I could hold it in any longer than that."

"I didn't think you could." He smirks and kisses me on the lips.

"Are you going to do something with that cock of yours, or just keep stroking it under the blankets?" I finally ask.

"I was hoping you'd climb on for a ride." He smirks.

"I'd be happy to," I say as I push him onto his back. I straddle his hips, lining up and sinking down onto his cock. The way he instantly fills me up never ceases to amaze me. "God, yes," I cry out when he's fully seated.

"What do you need this morning, slow and sensual or hard and fast?" Ryker asks as he pulls me in for a kiss.

Our movements complement each other. He thrusts up as my hips fall, giving me the pressure I desperately need.

I ride him until my legs give out, my stamina nothing like his. "Roll over, baby," he instructs, and I do so. He moves off the bed, standing at the edge, and pulls me to the edge. He places my ankles on his shoulders and thrusts inside of me, hitting me even deeper with this new angle.

"Yes yes yes," I chant as he hits the perfect spot with each and every thrust of his hips. The way he can keep his rhythm as he expertly swivels his hips has my eyes rolling back in my head as I come apart at his doing.

"That's it, baby, milk my cock for every last drop. Before you know it, I'll be putting a baby inside of you," he says before slamming into me one last time, his own orgasm hitting his body hard.

"You want that?" I ask, once we've both had a chance to catch our breaths.

"What?" he asks, looking up at me.

"A baby," I state.

"With you, absolutely. I see how amazing you are with Ellie and can only imagine how you'd be with a baby of our own."

"It will be like starting over for you," I remind him.

"And I'm okay with that. Nothing against my daughter, she's pretty amazing, but I want it all with you, as long as it's what you want. I don't want you to miss out on any of your dreams because I've already fulfilled some of them."

"I love you," I tell him.

"I love you, too, Aves," he says, calling me by the nickname only he uses.

"Can we wait until after we're married to do the whole baby thing? I want to be able to enjoy our wedding and honeymoon without having to worry about a pregnancy mixed in."

"Whenever you're ready for the baby-making, I'll be happy to oblige. Until then, we'll just have fun practicing." He winks and drops a kiss on my abdomen before standing all the way up and pulling out of me. "I need to shower and get some food in me before I take off for a few hours. Care to join me?"

"Always," I tell him, accepting the hand he's holding out for me to take. I'd follow this man anywhere he wants to go.

I LOOK DOWN at the sparkly diamond rings in the case. There are so many to choose from. "Can I try that one?" I ask the saleslady.

"Of course," she says as she unlocks the case and pulls it out. I slip it on my finger but can tell right away it isn't right for me, so I hand it back. "Do you have any preferences on cut or style of ring? Maybe I can point out something specific," she offers.

"I'd like a lower profile. I'm afraid if it sticks up too much, I'll bang it on everything, and I don't want to break it."

"I can understand the worry," she says as she checks the cases and pulls out a few options for me to try on. "We can also design a custom ring if you don't find anything you love. It takes about a week for them to come in."

"How does that process work?" Ryker asks her.

"We have some standard settings you can start

with, and then change things to your liking, along with choosing specific stone sizes and the clarity you want from the stone."

"Do you want to do that, babe?" Ryker asks as he stands behind me and looks over my shoulder as I try the rings on.

"I don't know yet. Let me try on a few more, and then we can decide," I tell him, flashing a quick smile over my shoulder at him.

"Whatever you want, babe," he says and kisses my cheek.

I try on what feels like every ring they have in the place and still haven't found something I love. I'm a little worried about custom ordering because what if I don't like the way it fits or looks, and then I'm stuck with a custom ring I hate.

"I just remembered we have a special collection in the back. Let me see if there's anything that might work for you," the saleslady says before stepping away to check.

"We can always try another store, if you want," Ryker tells me.

"I'm just so overwhelmed, at this point. I like a couple of them but was hoping I'd get that feeling, like, this is the one, as soon as I slip it on my finger."

"Then, try on a thousand of them until you get it," he says.

"I think you're going to love one of these," the lady says as she returns with two more rings. The first one she hands me is gorgeous, and I love the way the diamonds sparkle when the light hits them.

I take the ring from her and slide it on my finger. That moment I was just telling Ryker about is finally here. "This is it," I gasp. I can feel the tears start to prick my eyes as my emotions hit me.

"We'll take it," Ryker tells the saleslady. "Does it have a matching wedding band?" he asks.

"There are a few options," she tells him and pulls out another tray with them. We look together and I try them on one at a time to see how they look with the engagement ring.

"Oh, I love this one," I say as I put the third option on. It wraps around the band, adding a band on each side of the engagement ring.

"Then, we'll go with that one," Ryker says.

"How about you, sir. Did you want to try on wedding bands today, as well?" she asks.

"Oh, sure." He stammers just a bit.

"Let me show you the groom ones from the same collection," she says before stepping away again to bring those to us. Ryker tries on a couple of options, settling with a platinum band with a row of channel-set diamonds in it.

"How's the ring fitting?" she asks me, now that I've had a little bit of time to wear it. "Does it feel loose or too tight? We can send it to be resized, if necessary. Or you can wear it for a few days and decide."

"It actually feels good," I say as I spin it around my finger. "It doesn't feel tight but also doesn't feel like it is going to fall off if I shake my hand."

"Perfect. If something changes, just bring it back and we can have it fixed. The extended plan we recommend everyone purchase covers the cost of any resizing, and replacement of any stones that fall out or get damaged. If a setting breaks, it covers that cost, as well."

"Sounds good," I agree with her.

"Does that cover all of the rings?" Ryker asks.

"Yes, sir. We register each of them with pictures in the system. You can take them to any location, and they can find the purchase in our system to facilitate the claim."

"Perfect," he says, and holds out his credit card for the lady to take.

"Did you want me to box up the wedding bands?" she asks as she takes the rings from us to scan into her computer.

"That would be great, thank you," I say.

Twenty minutes later, we're walking out of the store, bag in Ryker's hand while I walk out with the engagement ring on my left ring finger.

"I still can't believe we're getting married," I giddily state as I hold my hand up and look at the sparkly diamond on my finger.

"Believe it, babe. There's no getting rid of me, now." He winks at me.

"I'd never want to get rid of you," I tell him.

"That's good to know. Means when I mess up, I don't have to worry about sleeping in Max's kennel with him."

I laugh at the thought of him in the kennel with Max. "Oh, we can still arrange for that," I tell him.

"Speaking of bedrooms and such, what do you say about going house hunting this week?"

"Oh, I guess we can do that."

"I know I just bought the condo last summer, but if we're going to be getting married and expanding our family, we're going to need more space, so there's no better time than now to start our search. We can keep the condos and rent them out, or put them up for sale, whatever you want to do."

"Keeping them as rentals isn't a bad idea. We can start looking online tonight and contact a realtor when we find something we want to look at," I suggest.

"Perfect, and if we can stay within the area so Ellie's close to school, it would be even better. I know it won't matter much once she's driving, here, soon," he says and trails off.

"What," I ask as he starts to go ghostly white.

"It's just hitting me. My daughter is growing up. She'll be sixteen and driving, soon. That means prom and graduation aren't all that far off, and I don't know if I'm ready for all of it."

I can't help but laugh at his antics. "You'll be fine, old man." I smirk as I call him that.

"Someone finally agrees with me; I'm getting old."

"You are not," I volley back.

"Are you sure you want to be with an old man like me?" he asks, but I know he isn't serious.

"Every day for the rest of my life," I tell him, and mean every word.

"You know it means that we might have to move to a new state if I'm traded or sign with a new team, right."

"Ryker, I'd follow you to the moon if it meant I got to be with you for the rest of my life. I don't care where we live. As long as we're together, I'll be the happiest woman on earth."

He brings my hand to his lips, pressing a kiss to the back of my hand, then one to my ring finger. "Okay, let's go tell our girl our news."

"Ellie, you home?" Ryker calls out when we get back.

"Yeah, I'm right here," she says from the couch. "Where's the fire?" she asks, giving her dad shit for how animated he's being.

"No fire, but Avery said yes and we're moving!" he blurts out.

"What?" Ellie says, jumping up from the couch.

I can't help but laugh at how the exchange is going.

"What your dad was trying to say is he asked me to marry him last night and I said yes. Then, today, we discussed finding a house we can move to, rather than staying here in the condo."

"Oh my god, yes! Have you picked a date yet? Can I see your ring? Why didn't you tell me you were going to ask her?" Ellie asks without taking a breath.

"I wasn't planning on asking until I had a ring, but the moment was right, so I went with it. We just got back from the jewelry store," he says, holding up the bag with the wedding bands. I hold up my hand so she can see my engagement ring. She quickly comes around the couch so she can get a better look.

"Wow, you picked a good one," she compliments. "Nice job, Dad."

"I had nothing to do with picking it out. Avery and the sales lady did all the picking."

"Semantics," she says, waving him off.

"We haven't picked a date yet," I explain. "I need a few days to wrap my mind around the idea, and so we can tell those that are important to us, like you. I haven't even told my parents or Tori yet. We wanted you to be the first to know."

"Really?" Ellie lights up and walks into my arms, hugging me tightly.

"I couldn't have picked a better woman for my dad than you. Thank you for making him so happy." Tears immediately spring to my eyes at her words. I know many stepmoms and stepdaughters butt heads and don't get along, so I'm very thankful Ellie and I get along so well.

"Thank you, Ellie. I love you like you are my own, and that won't ever change."

"Is someone cutting onions in here?" Ryker asks as he wraps his arms around both of us.

"No, but it's okay to let your emotional side show. We won't tell any of your teammates you cried with us," Ellie teases him. "Wouldn't want you to lose any of your badassery you have out on the ice."

He just rolls his eyes and pulls her head closer to him so he can place a kiss on her temple. "Love you, kiddo."

"Love you, too, Dad," she says before pulling from our embrace. "Can I help look for the house?" she asks.

"Of course," I tell her as I follow her to the couch. I grab my iPad as I do and pull up house listings online. "We should start a list of must-haves and wants so I can narrow things down."

"Five bedrooms, three, maybe four bathrooms, four-car garage, backyard for Max," Ryker starts tossing out.

"Five bedrooms? Why so many?" Ellie asks.

"One for us, you, an office for Avery, a guest room, and a baby's room."

"Wait—are you having a baby!?" Ellie asks, getting all excited.

"No, I'm not pregnant, but it's something we've talked about, but won't happen until after we're married," I'm quick to tell her.

"Oh." She deflates. "I was hoping for a sibling before I graduated and move out of the house."

"Convince her to marry me this year and we can see what we can do," Ryker tells her.

"Avery, can you please marry my dad this year?" Ellie turns to me, puppy dog eyes and everything.

"I'll see what I can do," I tell her for now. I just love how much she wants this for us. I couldn't imagine it being any other way.

CHAPTER 22

Ryker

"WHAT DO YOU NEED FROM ME?" I ask Avery as we look over the information the resort sent for their wedding packages.

"Talk to Jason and make sure they won't be pissed if we get married days after he does. I don't want to steal their thunder," she says.

"I don't think it will be a problem, but I'll double-check. It is just too perfect of a scenario for us to pass it up," I tell her.

The same venue Olivia and Jason are getting married at happened to have an opening for a wedding the follow weekend. Avery's just worried they'll be mad if we book it. I see it as killing two birds with one stone. A good chunk of our friends will already be in Hawaii for their wedding and can just stay for ours. Make it a nice week-long vacation.

I pick up my cell and hit Jason's contact, putting

the call on speaker so Avery can listen in to our conversation.

"Hey, Cap, how's it going?" he asks.

"I can't complain. How's it going for you? Did you guys make it back to Indy?"

"Yep, got here a few days ago. We went to see Olivia's parents, first, and then came here."

"Awesome. Is she around, by chance? I have a question for both of you."

"Yeah, let me grab her quick," he says, and I can hear him calling her name. "Okay, we're both here and on speaker, what's up?"

"As you may have heard, Avery and I are getting married. We're trying to pull it off before the start of the season. Where the two of you come in is, the resort in Hawaii has an opening the Friday after your wedding we can book. Avery was worried we'd be stealing your thunder, but I look at it as the perfect timing, as most of the guys will already be there for your wedding and can stick around for ours. So, she insisted I ask you guys before we sign the contract."

"Do it! You won't be stealing anything from us! I'm so excited for you guys," Olivia says. "Tell Avery to call me if she wants any help planning."

"Hear that, babe?" I say to Avery. "We're getting married in August." I smirk at her.

"Seriously, call me, Avery," Olivia says. "I can give you all my info on the resort and who to ask for when calling places."

"Thank you. I'm already feeling so overwhelmed with it all. Three months to plan a wedding isn't very long."

"It isn't, but the resort has an entire staff to help with weddings, so they'll take care of so much of it for you. I would, however, suggest going dress shopping ASAP. There were so many I couldn't even consider because the lead time required was months long."

"That is crazy, but we plan to go this weekend. I'm going with my mom, Ellie, and my best friend, Tori."

"Sounds fun! Maybe we can plan a joint bachelorette party?" Olivia suggests.

"That would be super fun, especially for all the WAGs."

"Exactly. So, once you have some free time, call me and we'll chat everything wedding-related."

"Will do, thanks!" Avery tells her.

"Sounds like we've got some bachelor parties to plan," Jason says.

"Something like that," I agree. We shoot the shit for a few more minutes before ending our call.

"Are you ready to sign the contract, now?" I ask Avery.

"I am," she says as she checks the different boxes on the contract, selecting the things she wants. "Did you want to look over any of this?"

"I can, but I'm just going to agree with whatever

it is that you've selected. I don't care what color the flowers are, or what the bows on the chairs look like. All I care about is I get to stand at the end of an aisle, have you walk to me, pledge our lives to one another and then dance the night away as we celebrate our love with our friends and family. I'll put on whatever suit or tux you tell me to, and probably have to hold back the urges to rip your dress off of you all night because I'll be hard the entire time you're in it."

Avery just shakes her head as she laughs at me. "You're worse than a sixteen-year-old boy, sometimes."

"Only for you." I smirk at her. "And I haven't heard any complaints, yet."

"No complaints, definitely no complaints coming from me." Her heated gaze tells me just how satisfied I leave her each time.

"Okay, sign here and here," she instructs, handing me the contract.

"Will they take a credit card, or do I need to wire the money?" I ask.

"I'll find out, but you know my parents are going to throw a fit about you paying for it."

"That's why I'll pay before they even know there's a balance due. This place isn't cheap, and I don't want them worrying about it." I tell her. "I—we can afford it, so please don't let them stress over it."

"I think I can appease them if I let them pay for my dress," she says.

"Perfect. I can agree to that, as long as you promise me you won't stress over the cost of your dress, and you'll let me pay the difference from what they can cover and the final cost if the one you pick is more than they can afford."

"I suppose I can agree to those terms," she states.

With the contract signed and submitted, I pull Avery into my arms, kissing her tenderly.

"Mrs. Avery Jorgensen has a nice ring to it," I say before kissing her once again.

"It sure does, Mr. Jorgensen."

"Love you, Aves."

Epilogue

AVERY

I SIT at the head table, looking out at the group of people here to celebrate our rehearsal with us. This week has been filled with so many parties. I was worried it would be too much, but it's been perfect.

"Ugh, he's going to drive me to drink," Tori whisper-yells next to me.

"Who is?" I ask.

"Aiden. Who else has been up my ass all week?" she deadpans.

"Girl, you just need to give in to his charm. I'm telling you, that man wants you."

"That's nice, but I don't date players."

"Why are you so convinced he's a player?" I ask. I've gotten to know Aiden, some, over the season, and he's sweet once you get to know him, but he does have a confident personality that can come off as cocky.

"Because he's always flirting with all the women in the room and can't believe I won't just drop my panties at his feet. I'm not just another notch for his bedpost."

"I think you should give him a chance. I think you'll be pleasantly surprised."

"I think you're just love-blind. Ryker has you so sex drunk you can't see what's actually happening out here in the real world."

"I can see clearly, thank you very much," I state before taking a drink of my champagne.

"Yeah, yeah." She rolls her eyes at me.

"Just dance with him once, and if you can honestly say he isn't a gentleman, then I'll stop encouraging you to give him a chance."

She looks me over, for a moment. "Fine, deal," she says and shakes my hand.

Aiden better man up and not screw this up. I've just handed him my best friend on a silver platter, one he's been trying to get for months now.

I sit in a chair in the salon, my hair is being pinned up by the stylist, while the rest of my bridal party is also being attended to.

"Avery, look this way," our photographer calls out, and I do as asked. My smile is instant. I don't think it has left my face this entire week.

We kicked off our time in Hawaii by watching Olivia and Jason pledge their lives to one another, followed by a week of fun activities leading up to our big day. We're getting married at sunset, but taking pictures before then to capture the beauty of the island.

"Beautiful!" she calls out after looking at her camera screen. "Once everyone is done in here, I'll follow you back into the suite to capture you getting into your dresses, and then I'll head out to set up the first look."

"Thank you, Heather," I call out. Olivia used the same photographer, and she was amazing for their wedding. The sneak peek images she's already released from their day has me so excited to see what she captures from ours. Having a friend get married at the same place, not even a full week before me, was something I worried about, but it turned out to be the best thing ever.

"You are the most beautiful bride!" Tori says once we're done with hair and makeup. "Ryker is going to be beside himself when he sees you."

"You think so?" I ask.

"Girl, please. You could show up in a trash bag with unwashed bedhead and the man would still fall at your damn feet."

"She isn't lying," Ellie chimes in. "My dad is so far gone for you. It's funny to catch him when he's daydreaming about you. Like a love-struck puppy."

"Don't let him hear you call him that," I tease Ellie.

"Oh, I've said it directly to him and he just smiles."

"Of course, he does." I roll my eyes just thinking of Ryker. My insides flutter at the thought of seeing him in a few minutes. I've seen him in a suit many times, but there's just something special about seeing him in the suit we picked out for the wedding.

"Are you ready to go see your man?" Heather asks.

"Absolutely!" I tell her.

"Then, follow me, I've already got him in place."

Ellie and I follow her out the door. We asked for our first look to be intimate. We don't want our special moment shared with everyone.

"Ryker is down at the arch, his back is to the aisle, so he won't see you approaching. I'm going to have Ellie go first, get those shots, and then have her step aside, then he'll turn his back again and it will be your turn to walk down. I'll grab a few shots of you walking toward him. Once you reach him, I'll have you place a hand on his shoulder, we'll get a few shots like that and then he'll turn around. Don't worry about what I'm doing, we'll get it all captured," Heather says.

"Okay, I think I can remember all of that," I tell her before blowing out a big breath.

I watch as Ellie walks down. The love between her and Ryker has tears springing to my eyes. He wasn't lying, the many times he's told me he lucked out when it came to hitting the kid lottery with Ellie. She's a teenager, so there are always those moments when we have to be the parents and put our foot down, but that doesn't happen often with her, at all.

I continue to watch them have their moment, and I'm thankful we decided to include her in this. I know her importance in Ryker's life, and I don't ever want to diminish that.

I dab at my eyes, hoping I haven't screwed up my makeup after watching their emotional moment. Heather gives me the cue; she's ready for me to walk out to him. I take in a calming breath and walk toward my future.

Ryker

I STAND FACING THE OCEAN, my eyes locked on the endless amount of water. I know Avery is getting closer to me, I can feel her presence in my soul. The moment her hand rests on my shoulder, a calmness settles in. She's here. She's about to be mine forever.

I cover her hand with my own, linking our fingers together while we wait for the cue I can turn around. I have no clue what her dress is going to look like, but it doesn't matter to me. She could walk out in a paper bag, and I'd still think she was beautiful and want to marry her today.

"I love you," I tell her as we stand here waiting.

"You can turn around, Ryker," Heather calls out. I don't hesitate another second. I want my eyes on my bride. I hold her hand as I spin around, the breath leaving my lungs at the exquisite woman standing before me. The way her body is showcased in her dress, it is almost as if the dress was made specifically for her.

"Absolute perfection," I whisper as I pull her into me, our foreheads coming together. "You are the most beautiful bride I've ever seen, and you're all mine," I tell her before I kiss her. I do my best to keep it gentle, so I don't mess up her makeup.

"You don't look so bad yourself," she whispers against my lips.

"Avery, can you turn to face me and lean into Ryker's embrace," Heather calls out.

We follow her instructions, allowing her to capture all the shots she needs. We add in family and the wedding party, as needed, ending only just a few minutes before the ceremony is scheduled to start.

The next hour goes by in the blink of an eye. Before I know it, I'm back under the flower-covered arch, with Avery and her dad walking my way. Even though I've seen her, touched her, and tasted her lips today, the sight of her walking to me takes my breath away. I don't know what I did in this lifetime to deserve her, but I'd do it all over again if it meant I'd get this moment and this woman to love for the rest of my life.

READY TO HEAD BACK to San Francisco? Aiden and Victoria are up next in Aiden ~ Available now!

Coming Soon

Tristan
San Francisco Shockwaves Book 3
Spring 2023
Pre-Order on your favorite retailer today!
Add on Goodreads today!

Acknowledgments

I have so many people to thank that I sometimes don't know where to start. I'll start with my family. Thank you for encouraging me to write all these stories that keep me up at night. Thank you for all the time you give me to hide away and type all the words!

Renee - I seriously couldn't do this without you! It is crazy sometimes how alike we think!

Jess Birks - Thank you for picking the winning name for the series! I loved involving my reader group, and loved your suggestion! It fit perfectly!

My multiple author group chats - Procrastinating & Butt Stuff, Chat full of Mommies, OG Girls - Thank you for all the laughs, sprints, and words of encouragement.

My readers! You are the real MVPs here! Thank you for reading my books and loving my characters just as much as I do.

xoxo,

Samantha

Also by Samantha Lind

INDIANAPOLIS EAGLES SERIES

Just Say Yes ~ Scoring The Player

Playing For Keeps ~ Protecting Her Heart

Against The Boards ~ The First Intermission

The Hardest Shot ~ The Game Changer

Rookie Move ~ The Final Period

Box Set 1 {Books 1-3} ~ Box Set 2 {Books 4-6}

INDIANAPOLIS LIGHTNING SERIES

The Perfect Pitch ~ The Curve Ball

The Screw Ball ~ The Change Up

LYRICS & LOVE SERIES

Marry Me ~ Drunk Girl

Rumor Going 'Round ~ Just A Kiss

STANDALONE TITLES

Tempting Tessa

Until You ~ An Aurora Rose Reynolds Happily Ever Alpha Crossover Novella

Until Her Smile ~ An Aurora Rose Reynolds Happily Ever Alpha Crossover Novel

Cocky Doc ~ A Cocky Hero Club Novel

Sweet valley, Tennessee

Nothing Bundt Love

Nothing Bundt Forever

San Francisco Shockwaves

Ryker

Aiden

Tristan

About the Author

Samantha Lind is a *USA TODAY* Bestselling contemporary romance author. When she's not dreaming up new stories, she can often be found with her family, traveling, reading, watching her boys on the ice or watching her favorite professional team (Go Knights Go!).

Connect with Samantha in the following places:

www.samanthalind.com
samantha@samanthalind.com

Reader Group
Samantha Lind's Alpha Loving Ladies
Good Reads
https://goo.gl/t3R9Vm
Newsletter
https://bit.ly/FDSLNL

facebook.com/SamanthaLindAuthor
x.com/samanthalind1
instagram.com/samanthalindauthor

Made in the USA
Columbia, SC
07 October 2024

43837173R00152